His Perfect Bride

By Merry Farmer

HIS PERFECT BRIDE

Cover design by Erin Dameron-Hill (the miracle-worker)
Embellishment by © Olgasha | Dreamstime.com

ASIN: B019UBPGSU
Paperback:
ISBN-13: 9781522903727
ISBN-10: 1522903720

If you'd like to be the first to learn about when the next books in the series come out and more, please sign up for my newsletter here: http://eepurl.com/RQ-KX

Like historical western romance? Come join us in the Pioneer Hearts group on Facebook for games, prizes, exclusive content, and first looks at the latest releases of your favorite historical western authors. https://www.facebook.com/groups/pioneerhearts/

To all the wonderful ladies of Pioneer Hearts,
who inspired me to take on the wonderful world
of mail-order brides. Enjoy!

Table of Contents

Chapter One

Haskell, Wyoming – 1875

Haskell, Wyoming was like any other frontier town in that it was made up of a few rows of new buildings surrounded by vast stretches of farm and ranch land, and overlooked by majestic mountains. Like a few other, lucky frontier towns, the railroad connected it to larger cities and the bustling industry of the West Coast.

But what made Haskell different from every other town in the foothills of the Rockies was that it was inhabited by the strangest collection of thinkers, dreamers, and doers west of the Mississippi. Maybe it was the fact that Howard Haskell—who co-owned Paradise Ranch with his sister, Virginia Piedmont—had woken up one day and decided to build a town out of nothing, just the way he wanted it. Maybe it was the intrepid families—many of whom had traveled west on the Oregon Trail along with Howard's daughter, Lucy, a decade before—who first settled in the town and still formed its core. Or maybe it was simply the fresh, Wyoming air, and the sunshine that danced across the grasslands and shone off the snow-capped mountains. It gave inhabitants and visitors to the town alike a sense that anything was possible in Haskell.

Anything was possible, which was exactly why Mr. Charlie Garrett, owner of the Cattleman Hotel, the Silver Dollar Saloon, and the town's school, invited Virginia Piedmont and her close friend, Mrs. Josephine Evans, to brunch on a balmy spring morning.

"Ladies, I have an idea I wanted to run past you," Charlie said, striding into the hotel's dining room. Charlie wore an expertly tailored suit, the fob of his gold pocket watch showing against his vest. His dark hair was carefully groomed. The only thing that interrupted the image of a wealthy and powerful man of charm and poise was the equally well-dressed two-year-old girl he carried in one arm and her twin brother in the other.

"Good morning, Miss Ellen." Josephine rose from her seat at a table by the window to reach for Charlie's daughter. "And you too, Master Allen." She leaned forward to kiss the boy's forehead.

Virginia hopped up to claim Allen. The two cuddled like old friends—indeed, Virginia and Josephine were considered to be grandmas to everyone in Haskell—before sitting at the table. Virginia promptly handed Allen a buttered biscuit, then said, "This idea of yours had better be more than the two of us babysitting for you, Charlie."

Charlie joined the women at the table with a laugh and a smile. "Oh, it's much more than that."

"Well?" Josephine prompted, settling Ellen on her lap and handing her a strawberry. "I'm all ears. We've been speculating about what you want all morning."

Virginia nodded and hummed in agreement. "Spill it."

Charlie chuckled, mostly because Allen lunged toward the table, reaching for Virginia's teacup right as she spoke. "I'd be careful about what you say with that wiggle worm in your lap. He takes after his mother and will do anything you ask him to do twice as well as you expected it to be done."

"Me?" Allen asked, all toddler innocence.

"Yes, you, my boy." Charlie reached across to poke his tummy, sending Allen into giggles. "And your mother, which is why I'm here."

He took a breath, settled back in his chair, and rolled his shoulders. "The other night, Olivia and I were going over some business regarding my dear, old friend and mentor, Josiah Hurst's estate. You know that among many of the other charitable institutions he left behind when he passed on, one of them is a home for women who have been battered or abused or otherwise escaped from dangerous situations."

"Hurst Home." Josephine nodded. "You are truly a saint for setting up such a wonderful, safe place for those women."

"Well, it was Olivia's idea as much as mine," Charlie insisted.

"Either way, it warms my heart to know that there's a safe place for those poor women to go in troubled times," Virginia added.

"Exactly," Charlie continued. "That's what set Olivia to thinking the other night. Some of the stories of the women currently living at Hurst Home would break your heart. They've endured so much, and even though the home is a safe place for them, Olivia had the idea that it would be even safer for some of them to start new lives far, far away from the troubles of their pasts."

"New lives?" Josephine exchanged a glance with Ellen...who was more interested in the cup of fruit at Josephine's place than the conversation. "How so?"

Charlie leaned forward. "Olivia was reading a newspaper that her mother sent her from back home in Ohio. Among its pages, she noticed an advertisement by a miner over in Colorado, looking for a wife."

"Ah, mail-order brides." Virginia nodded. "I hear that quite a few men who have settled out here are sending back East for wives these days."

"Which brings me to my point." Charlie smiled. "Olivia and I feel as though it would benefit a great deal of people if we could find a way to bring some of the women from Hurst Home out here, to Haskell, to be brides for the young men working at Paradise Ranch, or in town, or on any of the other ranches in the area."

Josephine and Virginia hummed and exchanged looks of surprise and interest.

"Well, it would certainly stop so many of them from patronizing Bonnie's all the time," Josephine said.

"Very true." Virginia nodded slowly. "I'm not saying Bonnie Horner wasn't smart to open a whorehouse in Haskell."

"She certainly did cut down on the amount of mischief all those virile, young ranch hands got into," Josephine added with a wry drawl.

"Mmm." Virginia arched an eyebrow. "Several of those boys are far more grown up now than they were when Bonnie opened her doors. It's about time they settled down and started families."

"The only way for Haskell to grow is by welcoming families and inviting them to put down roots," Josephine agreed.

The two women turned to Charlie once more.

"I see we're in agreement." Charlie winked. "And I think Bonnie would agree with us too, at heart."

"She's got other irons in the fire, that Bonnie,"

Virginia said, exchanging a knowing look with Josephine.

"So are we agreed?" Charlie asked. "Should we send a telegraph to Mrs. Breashears at Hurst Home asking how she feels about the plan?"

"Absolutely," Josephine said.

"The sooner the better," Virginia agreed.

"Excellent." Charlie smiled and tapped the table to seal the deal. "Now all we have to do is figure out which lucky man should be our trial groom." He twisted to wave across the hotel dining room, catching the eye of the stately, white-haired man standing ramrod straight near the doorway to the lobby.

The white-haired man nodded and glided across the room to the table. "Can I help you, Mr. Garrett?"

"Yes, Gunn. Breakfast for my two sweet angels." He winked across the table to Ellen, and reached to his side to ruffle Allen's hair. "And anything else that Mrs. Piedmont and Mrs. Evans want."

"Right away, sir." Mr. Gunn bowed and moved off.

"What about Theophilus Gunn?" Josephine whispered as the gentleman walked away. "He's getting up in years and could use a wife."

Charlie shook his head and chuckled.

Virginia laughed outright. "Mr. Gunn is far too long in the tooth for any of the young ladies of Hurst Home. Besides, to hear Charlie tell it, he's married to his job."

"Best hotel manager Wyoming has ever seen," Charlie agreed. "And Virginia is right. We need to think younger. What young man in Haskell do we know who needs a bride?"

"And who is mature and kind enough to treat a woman who has been through the wringer well," Josephine added.

The three of them sat back in silence, mulling over the

question. Charlie rubbed his chin, studying his babies. They were too young by ages to even thing about marriage, as were his two older children, but he still put himself in the position of the father of a daughter in need of a mate. Which young men in town would he most trust with a tender heart?

One of Mr. Gunn's waitresses returned with a breakfast tray, laying all manner of delicacies out for them as Gunn stood to the side, watching and waiting. Children and grown-ups alike dove in. It was easier to think on a full stomach.

"You know who I have wanted to find a good woman and settle down for years?" Virginia began as the last of the cream tarts and bacon was devoured.

"Who?" Charlie dabbed his mouth, then put down his napkin, ready for business.

Virginia hesitated before saying, "My nephew, Franklin."

A wave of uncertain excitement swept over the table. Franklin Haskell. Yes. He was Howard Haskell's son, not to mention Howard's right-hand man on the ranch. Franklin more or less ran things, now that Howard's interests had turned to building a unique town and helping it to thrive. But all Charlie really knew about Franklin was that he was quiet, serious, and a cripple.

"You know, Franklin *could* use a wife," Josephine agreed.

"Mmm." Virginia nodded, smoothing a hand across Allen's head as he rested against her chest and closed his eyes for a nap. "But will he see things that way?"

"He's close to thirty now," Josephine reasoned. "I know he'll argue he's been doing well on his own since Gideon Faraday constructed those braces for him, but there's something so sad about him, so haunted."

"There is," Virginia agreed. "And I know what it is. You weren't here when he had that accident that crushed and sliced up his legs. I was. He won't let it go."

"But that was ten…eleven years ago," Charlie said. "Surely he can move on by now."

Virginia let out a breath. "Franklin is tricky. He hasn't been the same since that accident. There's more going on in his head than he lets on, and I don't think all of it is good."

"And you think a wife would help?" Charlie asked.

"A very special wife, yes." Virginia nodded, then tilted her head to the side in thought. "She would have to be an exceptional woman, though—patient, kind, strong. We would need to ask Mrs. Breashears to send us the very best she has."

"I think that could be arranged." Charlie nodded.

"That settles it, then." Josephine let Ellen wiggle down from her lap and cross around the table to her father. "Franklin will get the first and best wife."

Charlie scooped Ellen into his arms. "If he agrees."

"There's only one way to find out," Virginia said. "We'll have to ask him."

Three hours later, the twins safe at home with Muriel Chance watching them, Charlie, Virginia, and Josephine rode through the gates of Paradise Ranch. The ranch was only a short drive from town. Howard was a man of vision and had planned the town and the ranch so that they could grow together over the years. Right now, the town was two miles away from the ranch's property line, with a neighborhood of houses under construction midway between the two. Howard's house was set a mile into the ranch, Virginia's another mile further on. A bunkhouse and several outbuildings were clustered close to each of the big houses to provide for the two teams of ranch hands that worked—sometimes together, sometimes in friendly competition—to maintain the herd.

Franklin's house was midway between Howard's and Virginia's, separated on either side by grassland and a stream. Howard had argued for weeks about his son building a house so far from anyone else, but Franklin was stubborn. Charlie had to admit as he pulled his wagon to a stop in the yard that Franklin had an eye for placement. Separated though is house was, it was surrounded by beauty, calm, and quiet.

"Franklin," Virginia marched ahead as Charlie helped Josephine down from the wagon. "Are you home?"

The front door of Franklin's house and the windows were open to let in the spring breeze. Franklin was already on his way out to the porch as Charlie and the women approached. He moved slowly, walking onto the porch with stilted steps. The braces Gideon had constructed fit firmly over his calves with iron bands, had hinges by his knees, and clamped around his thighs to give him support. Even with that, he gripped the doorframe, and then the porch railing, as he came out to greet his visitors.

"Aunt Ginny." He nodded to Virginia without smiling. "Mrs. Evans, Mr. Garrett. What can I do for you?"

Serious to the bone. Charlie's heart went out to the young man. The weight Franklin carried on his shoulders was all but visible.

"Franklin, we've come with a proposition for you," Charlie began. More than ever, he wanted this to work out for the young man. Everyone deserved a little joy in their life, no matter what their past. His own dear Olivia had taught him that ten years ago, and continued to teach him every day.

"Oh?" As Charlie, Virginia, and Josephine reached

the porch, Franklin gestured to the bench and chairs. "What proposition?"

Normally Charlie would have remained standing, but clearly Franklin was uncomfortable. All four of them took seats and got down to business.

"I've told you about Hurst Home, haven't I?" Charlie began.

"It's that wonderful home for women who have been battered or are in danger," Josephine rushed on.

Franklin frowned, nodding. "In Nashville, right?"

"That's it," Charlie said.

"We want to start bringing some of those unfortunate young women out to Haskell, to marry men here," Virginia burst. Her eyes glowed with excitement.

Franklin paused, his frown shifting to consideration. "Sounds like a grand idea to me."

"Good, we hoped you'd think so." Josephine smiled and sat straighter.

"Because we'd like to start by finding a bride for you," Virginia finished her friend's thought.

Charlie cringed inwardly. That wasn't how he would have proceeded. Franklin looked as stunned as Charlie imagined he would be if he were in that position.

"You want to send away for a woman to be my wife," he said, shifting his baffled look from Josephine to Virginia and back.

The two women exchanged knowing grins, then said in unison, "Yes."

Silence. Charlie debated stepping in and calling the whole experiment off.

At last, Franklin drew in a long breath and shook his head. "I don't know. What woman in her right mind would want to be saddled with a..." He closed his mouth and swallowed, back going stiff. "With me?"

More awkward silence, then Virginia said, "You're looking at this all wrong, Franklin, I can tell."

Franklin set his jaw and fixed his aunt with a challenging look. "How am I looking at it?"

"I know you, my boy. I've known you my whole life," Virginia went on. "You're thinking that it would be a curse to trap a nice girl with a man who can't walk or run or gad about, like other men."

Franklin blinked. "Well, it would."

Virginia shook her head and brushed his protest aside with a wave. "First of all, that's bull—that's nonsense." Charlie grinned at Virginia's typical, unladylike speech. "Second of all, it's selfish."

"Selfish?" Franklin tensed further, the muscles of his broad shoulders rippling as if Virginia had hit a nerve.

"Selfish," Virginia repeated. "Look at things from the poor girls in that home's point of view. Their lives have been hard, horrible, even. They've been in far more danger than you or I ever have, endured more than, yes, even you."

Franklin let out a breath and scratched his thigh under the edge of the brace he wore. "Maybe."

"More than maybe, my boy." Virginia scooted to the edge of her seat and changed tactics, softening her voice. "Think about how wonderful it would be, how much it would change some poor woman's life, to come out to a peaceful, quiet, *safe* place like this. Think what a blessing it would be for her to marry a good, kind man who would never raise a hand or his voice to her when that may be all she's ever known."

Her words were so powerful that Charlie caught himself rubbing the sore spot of his heart under his vest.

"This may be the chance that makes all the difference to a woman," Virginia went on. "You could be exactly what some poor girl needs to feel whole again."

Franklin met her gaze, emotion making his eyes bright. In that moment, Charlie knew that Virginia had convinced him.

"I hadn't thought of it like that," he said, solemn and serious. He took a deep breath and sat straighter.

For several long moments he was silent, his far-away expression revealing thoughts that were busy sorting themselves out. They waited for those thoughts to come around, for Franklin to make his decision.

At last, with a soft sigh, Franklin nodded, the picture of resolve. "All right. I'll do it. You can send for a girl to come here and marry me. But I don't know how happy I'll be able to make her."

"Oh, I think you'll make her very happy." Virginia stood. She gestured for Charlie and Josephine to stand as well, though Charlie was inclined to stay and talk things out with Franklin a little more. "I think you'll make a lot of people happy with this decision," she went on, "yourself among them."

"If you say so." Franklin leaned back in his chair, looking as though he needed to sit there and ponder what he'd done a little longer.

"I'll drop by with the address for Hurst Home later so you can write to the girl," Charlie said.

He, Virginia, and Josephine headed back to the wagon.

"He's the sort who needs to be alone with his thoughts," Virginia explained as soon as they were driving out of earshot. "I know my nephew. This is a good decision for him, and the less we beat him over the head with it, the quicker he'll come to realize that."

"Now all we have to do is figure out which young

woman at Hurst Home would be right for him," Charlie said.

"Yes." Josephine took up the challenge right away. "She will have to be someone with enormous stores of patience."

"Right," Virginia agreed. "Someone with a head on her shoulders too."

"She'll have to be all right with a man who faces physical challenges," Charlie added uncertainly.

"Obviously." Virginia nodded. "And she'll have to be able to spend stretches of time by herself."

"True," Josephine said. "Franklin isn't a ranch hand and doesn't go on the drives with the others, but he still has quite a bit of work managing the ranch."

Charlie let out a laugh, tension easing from his shoulders. "Why, now that I think of it, Franklin Haskell is quite a catch for any girl. He's wealthy, sober, and respected. Why haven't any of the local girls set their cap for him yet?"

Josephine and Virginia exchanged another of those looks that only women could manage. "It's not that none of them have set their cap for him," Josephine began.

"It's that he hasn't been interested in any of them," Virginia finished.

Charlie frowned and sent the two a sideways look as he drove. "We're not bringing some sweet young girl into a situation where she'll have a rival, are we?"

Neither women answered right away.

"Not really," Josephine said at last. "Franklin hasn't shown a lick of interest."

"But there is a girl in town who is interested in him?" Charlie asked.

Virginia and Josephine remained silent.

Chapter Two

As the train whistle blew, its shrill sound competing with the squeal of brakes that signaled their final approach to the station in Haskell, Wyoming, Corva Collier clutched her paint box to her chest. This was it. Her heart raced at a thousand beats per minute as she took one final look out the window.

For days, she'd seen nothing but vast, empty space out the train window—first endless stretches of grassland and then wide plains with towering mountains all around. The expansive vistas filled with greens and browns, greys and purples that she'd only ever imagined when she mixed her paints, had captivated her. Every bend in the tracks had shown her a new picture, begged her to open her paints, lay out a canvas and translate the beauty into a captured moment. Of course, it was impossible to paint on a moving train packed with passengers, but it was not impossible to dream.

At last, after darkness and terror that she thought would never end, it was possible to dream.

Another sharp whistle shook her out of her thoughts. The open landscape—dotted here and there with herds of cattle or smaller groups of horses—gave way to a sudden and cheery town. The train lurched to a stop in front of a wooden platform. The wood was still a verdant light brown, suggesting the platform was new.

Corva smiled, telling her shoulders to unbunch. The West was new, Wyoming was new, and Haskell was newer still. Mrs. Breashears had explained this quaint town that had popped up on the whim of rancher Howard Haskell and his family, explained the dire need they had for women to marry the ranch hands and businessmen who had rushed to claim their corner of the booming enterprise. The prospect of settling somewhere far away from Nashville, far away from the nightmare of Atlanta as well, was all the incentive Corva needed. The sweet letter she'd received from Mr. Franklin Haskell, personally inviting her to come to Paradise Ranch to be his bride, was merely icing on the cake of her escape from a life that had felt like death itself.

As soon as the man who sat across the aisle from her stood and walked to the front of the car, Corva dipped into the pocket of her coat and took out a small, round mirror. She checked her hair, turned this way and that to study her face. The bruises that had constantly marred her complexion for most of her life had been gone for a year, but in her heart she expected to see them pop up again at any moment. That didn't mean she liked what she saw, though. She was nothing but a short, ugly, useless—

No. Those were Uncle Stanley's words, not hers. She closed her eyes, took a breath, and reminded herself that her uncle was in the past, and his temper was nothing but a few faded scars to her now. As those scars healed, her work—the work of believing in herself—had begun. Believing in herself was so much harder than she thought it would be.

"Miss, are you getting off here?" the conductor asked from the front of the car.

Corva cleared her throat. "Yes." Her voice was no more than a wisp. She stood, slipping the mirror back into her pocket and tightening her grip around the handle of her paint box. She moved to the aisle and twisted and reached for her carpetbag in the rack above the seat.

"I can help you with that." The conductor strode forward to fetch her bag. It was new and possibly the prettiest thing she owned, aside from the potential in her paints. Mrs. Breashears had purchased it especially for this journey.

"Thank you." All Corva could offer the kind conductor was a smile, but that seemed to be payment enough. He smiled in return—the way Corva imagined her long-departed father would have smiled at her—and preceded up the aisle to the door, bag in hand.

As she stepped down onto the platform in Haskell, Corva held her breath. Behind the scent of coal smoke and metal that was the train, she caught a whiff of freshly sawed wood, animal, and beyond that, something cleaner, purer. Men and women in every kind of dress from tailored suits to worn aprons, bustled against the backdrop of a town burgeoning with new life and the fresh colors of whitewash and painted shutters. Her gaze drifted to the mountains in the distance, their caps still snowy, even though it was late spring.

"Now, who's here to meet you, Miss Collier?" the conductor asked. "It would be irresponsible for me to turn a sweet thing like you off on your own."

Corva blushed and lowered her head, blinking rapidly. Sweet? Her? No one had ever called her sweet or taken any sort of interest in her at all. She opened her mouth to answer.

"Corva Collier? Miss Corva Collier?"

Corva and the conductor both turned to find a pair of grey-haired ladies in fine dresses with astounding bustles marching toward them.

"Yes, you must be Corva," the one on the right—slightly older than the other but as vibrant as a young girl—said. "Margaret Breashears said you were a painter." She nodded to the box Corva carried.

"Is that what that is?" the younger of the two said. She looked as full of life as a woman half her age. The word "trouble" popped to Corva's mind as she studied the two of them together.

"Yes," the first one said. "It's a paint box."

"Oh, how lovely."

"I'm Virginia Piedmont." The first woman thrust out her hand for Corva to shake.

"And I'm Josephine Evans." The second one followed suit.

It was then that Corva realized her mouth still hung open from the comment she'd been about to make to the conductor. She snapped it shut, blushing furiously, shifted her paint box to her left hand, then shook hands with both women, adding a quiet, "How do you do?" in her soft, Georgia accent.

"Well, now that you're here," Virginia said, beaming with satisfaction. She nodded to the carpetbag that the amused conductor still carried. "Is that all you brought with you?"

"Oh, no." Corva's heart leapt back to her throat as she glanced from the women to the train, and then pleadingly at the conductor.

The good man sensed her thoughts enough to say, "I'll fetch your crates, Miss Collier. Don't you worry."

"Crates?" Josephine asked as she reached to take the carpetbag from the conductor. "What crates?"

"You'll see." The conductor gave her a saucy wink, then hurried along to the last train car.

"I brought a few paintings with me," Corva explained. "I...I hope you don't mind."

"Mind?" Josephine laughed. "Why would I mind? That sounds delightful."

"It's really up to Franklin to mind," Virginia said.

"You're...you're his aunt, aren't you?" Corva asked. "At least, he mentioned an Aunt Virginia who was helping bring me here in his letter."

"Yes, dear." Virginia beamed. "That's me. It was nice of Franklin to remember me."

Josephine sucked in a breath and nodded, as if remembering something herself. Then the two women turned in unison to look behind them.

Corva looked as well, and pressed a hand to her stomach. There, standing just beyond the edge of the platform on the board sidewalk that stretched away down the town's main street, stood a man in a suit. Corva felt her cheeks go pink and her skin tingle with excitement and apprehension. The man was startlingly handsome, with dark hair and eyes so blue she could see them across the distance. He was clean-shaven and well-groomed, and the suit he wore was finely made and tailored to fit him perfectly. But what drew her attention were the iron braces on his legs—like twin cages—and the ivory-topped cane that he leaned against.

Franklin Haskell. Her groom.

The explosion of butterflies in her stomach made her head swim for a moment. Mrs. Franklin Haskell. How many times in the last few days had she repeated those words to see how they felt? Now, seeing the man himself, seeing those braces and…and yes, the sadness in his eyes, her heart thrummed with an intensity she hadn't expected. At first sight, her heart broke for the man.

"Mr. Haskell?" She pushed her nerves aside and crossed the platform, going to him since it was clear he wouldn't be able to rush to her.

"Yes." He nodded, unsmiling. His expression was kind in spite of that lack of smile. "Miss Collier?"

"Yes." She couldn't help the smile that came to her at the resonant sound of his voice. She held out her hand. He took it in a firm shake that filled her with confidence. "Thank you so much." The burst of emotion that tumbled out from her left her eyes stinging with tears and her cheeks hot with embarrassment. "You have no idea how much this means to me."

"I—" Whatever Franklin was about to say, he let it go, choosing to study her with his searching, blue eyes. At last, he swallowed, giving her hand—which he still held— a squeeze. "My pleasure."

He paused after those words, a masculine flush tinting his cheeks. Corva's mind raced through the paints she'd brought with her to blend that hue just right.

"Here you go, Miss Collier."

Corva dropped Franklin's hand and twisted to see the conductor carrying two tall, thin crates of her paintings forward. Each crate was three feet high with handles on the top, but neither was particularly heavy.

"Oh my," Josephine exclaimed, pressing a hand to her chest.

Virginia was too busy watching Corva and Franklin, touching a gloved hand to the corner of one eye.

"What are those?" Franklin asked.

A jolt of self-consciousness hit Corva. "A few paintings," she explained, lowering her gaze.

"I see."

"We can take those back to the ranch for you." Virginia launched into action. "Sir, my wagon is right over there, if you wouldn't mind bringing those over." She waved for the conductor to follow her to a row of parked wagons next to the platform.

"I'll take your bag, Miss Collier, and that box, if you don't mind." Josephine stepped up to Corva's side.

"Please call me Corva," she said, taking in Josephine, Virginia, and Franklin with a look.

"Such a pretty, unusual name." Josephine took her paint box, then rushed off with Virginia, leaving Corva and Franklin alone.

What did she say to a man she'd just met, a man who she had come to marry? There didn't seem to be any words. Corva steeled her courage and smiled up at Franklin. He certainly was handsome, in spite of the sadness in his eyes.

Franklin cleared his throat and offered Corva his free arm. "We should probably start over to the church. You may have guessed that I don't move as fast as most men."

"Oh." Corva reached for his arm, tucking her hand into his elbow. Was he joking or was he serious? It was hard to tell when he didn't smile. But no, there was a light in his eyes that told her he was at least trying to make light of things. The warmth and solidity of him next to her as they took one, slow step at a time away from the train, turning left and heading along a road that ran perpendicular to the street full of shops, gave her confidence.

"Aunt Ginny and Mrs. Evans, and even Mr. Garrett, all agree that it's best for us to be married right away," Franklin explained. "So that there's not any impropriety about you moving into my house."

"Yes, Mrs. Breashears explained as much," Corva said. "I don't mind. Not at all."

"Good." Franklin nodded.

Awkward silence fell between them as they passed in front of several buildings that smelled of new wood and fresh paint. They were mostly carpentry and metalwork shops, a leather and saddle store, and other manly occupations that seemed right at home alongside a railroad track. They turned right onto a road that ran parallel to the main street, which contained mostly new houses and, further along, a boarding house. At the end of that stretch, up a slight hill, on the edge of the tiny town, was a whitewashed church with a tall steeple containing a bell.

Corva's brow rose as they approached the church. "Are those stained glass windows?"

"They are." Franklin nodded. His lips twitched, although it wasn't quite a smile. "Some men spend their money on extravagant mansions or whirlwind tours of Europe. My father has spent his building a town, but he has…unusual tastes. He had these windows made back East and shipped out here eight years ago when the church was first built."

"They're beautiful."

Franklin hummed. "Wait until you see them from the inside."

He was right. It took him a minute or two to struggle up the three stairs that led to the church's front door, but once that was taken care of, he pushed the door open for her, revealing a world of dancing, colored light.

Corva sucked in a breath, leaving Franklin behind her for a moment to wander into the spacious chapel. Sunlight streamed through the stained glass, splashing bursts of red and green and purple against the white walls. Great care must have been taken with the placement of the church and each window, as the abstract designs of colored sunlight glittered perfectly against each wall. It was like stepping inside of a work of art.

"Funnily enough, we have extremely high church attendance in Haskell," Franklin spoke behind her.

"I can imagine." Corva breathed out the words. "This is the perfect place to worship the Lord."

She twisted to beam at Franklin, more certain than ever that she'd made the right decision in taking Mrs. Breashears up on her suggestion that she marry this man.

"Can I help you?" A voice at the front of the chapel snagged her attention before she could say anything.

A man in shirtsleeves and grey trousers stepped through a door at the side of the simple chancel at the front of the chapel.

"Rev. Pickering." Franklin resumed his slow stride up the church's center aisle.

Corva skipped back to take his arm and walk with him. It was her wedding march, after all.

"Ah, Franklin." The young reverend strode forward to meet the two of them at the front of the chapel. "Is this Miss Collier?"

Franklin turned to Corva, light in his eyes. "Yes."

"Good, good." The reverend clapped his hands together. "Well, I'm all ready. Are Mrs. Evans and your aunt Virginia going to join us as witnesses?"

"Yes," Josephine called from the back of the room, shooting through the church door, Virginia at her side. "We're here."

That was all that was needed. Rev. Pickering had known they were coming and made arrangements in advance. There was even a bouquet of daffodils for Corva and a veil, which she graciously declined. The beauty of the chapel was enough for her, though her artist's mind could barely contain itself through the short service.

Before Corva could catch her breath and wrap her mind around the importance of what she was doing, she was answering "I do," to Rev. Pickering's questions about whether she would love, honor, and cherish the man beside her, the man she'd just met. Franklin took his vows with heartfelt solemnity. Corva may not have known much about him, but beyond doubt, she was certain that he would never raise a hand to her. That was all that mattered.

"Then, by the power invested in me by our Lord and the territory of Wyoming, I pronounce you man and wife. You may kiss your bride."

As Rev. Pickering finished, Franklin turned to face Corva. With careful respect, he leaned toward her and touched his lips to hers. It was a formal kiss, but Corva had received so few kisses, so few embraces and kind words, in her life that she closed her eyes and savored it. Franklin was her husband and, as such, there would be more than kisses at some point, but for now, this was all she needed.

"Perfect, perfect." Virginia sighed beside them, dabbing at her eyes as if this was the culmination of a long love story. "Franklin, my boy, I'm proud of you."

To Corva's surprise, Franklin flushed red at the compliment, as if it was undeserved. "Thank *you*, Aunt Ginny."

Virginia shook her head. "Oh, now, none of that. You know I've always been proud of you."

"Always?" Franklin's comment was so quiet this time that Corva wasn't sure she'd heard it.

"Now. Shall we all go to the hotel? Introduce Corva to your friends and neighbors?" Josephine asked.

The prospect of being paraded in front of a bunch of strangers and clucked over didn't sit well with Corva.

Whether Franklin noticed the way she shrank at the prospect, or whether he already had other ideas in mind, he said, "If you don't mind, I'd rather take Corva back to the ranch to show her the house."

"Yes, of course, of course." Virginia waved her hand. "I need to head home and see how Jarvis is doing with the herd anyhow. We have at least a dozen cows who are about to calf," she explained to Corva.

"And if I don't get home and make sure lunch is taken care of, Pete will be a curmudgeon all afternoon," Josephine added.

"We sent your things on to the ranch with Luke, by the way," Virginia added. "Ran into him just outside the station. I hope you don't mind."

"Not at all," Franklin answered.

That was it. Within minutes, their small group had dispersed, and Corva found herself strolling along at a snail's pace with Franklin in the fresh outdoors once more.

"My wagon is parked at the hotel," he explained as they edged their way around the church's huge yard. "It's faster to cut through this way, and I can show you some of Haskell in the process."

Corva glanced this way and that, taking in everything as they walked—green fields, new buildings, and snow-capped mountains on the horizon. "It's such a picturesque town." It all but begged to be painted.

"My father's theory is that industry is only half of what draws people to settle in a certain place," Franklin explained. "Aesthetics and community are the rest."

"He may have a point."

"The church, for example," Franklin went on. "You saw how lovely it is. And the church yard."

"It's enormous."

Franklin nodded. "That's because we have a potluck lunch for the entire town after church each Sunday, when the weather permits. In fact, Dad wants to build a shelter of some sort so that we can have our potlucks in the rain too."

"How interesting."

"There's a town council, but honestly, almost every issue that crops up in Haskell is decided at potlucks through the course of conversation."

Corva grinned, giving the yard beside the church one last look. "I think I like that idea."

"It makes for some interesting lunches."

She laughed. Even though Franklin's expression remained impassive, laughter felt right.

A loud, popping crack ahead drew her attention on. Beyond the church yard was another, huge yard—a baseball field. It was lined with raised rows of benches on two sides. Several people sat in small clusters on those benches, watching as what looked like a single team practiced on the diamond.

"Baseball," Corva exclaimed. "I've heard so much about the game since the end of the war, but I've never seen it played."

Franklin nodded to the field. "You'll certainly get to see it played here. Haskell has gone nuts over the sport. Each of the surrounding ranches and the town have their own teams." He grew a shade more serious as he nodded toward the diamond and said, "That's the Bonneville Bears practicing right now."

"Bonneville Bears?"

His expression grew darker still as he said, "Rex Bonneville. He owns a ranch adjoining ours. The second biggest ranch in these parts. He's a bit—"

"Franklin!"

His explanation was cut off by a high-pitched, female shout. Corva had to search for a second before she spotted a short woman in a flouncy purple dress with honey-brown hair waving her arms at him. The woman had jumped up from a circle of three other young women, all of whom bore a distinct resemblance. The woman who had called out hopped down from one of the higher benches and charged across the field. The only hint Corva had of Franklin's feelings about the woman was a quick, heavy sigh.

"Franklin, what a treat to see you in town today. I wish you had told me you were coming in. I would have invited you to watch the boys practice with us. We're having such a jolly time." The flouncy woman finally puffed to a stop when she was mere feet from Franklin.

"Vivian." Franklin managed a tense pinch of his mouth, which may have been an attempt at a smile.

"You're looking dashing today," Vivian went on. "Is that a new suit? It looks expensive. Did it come in on the train just now? I simply love it when you or your family send away for fancy things that come in on the train."

A hitch formed in Corva's chest, not of jealousy—which part of her thought she should be feeling, considering how beautiful and fine the woman in front of her was—but of embarrassment for the woman's sake. She was well aware that men came west looking for gold, but apparently women did too.

"This isn't a new suit," Franklin said. He cleared his throat. "I did meet the train, however. I came to town to greet Corva when she arrived." He glanced to Corva.

Only then did Vivian blink and glance to Corva, noticing her existence. "Who's she?"

Franklin took his time answering. "Vivian, I'd like

you to meet Miss Corva Collier." He stopped, nodded to himself, then said, "I mean, Mrs. Corva Haskell."

A warm flush filled Corva's body. That was her name now, wasn't it? Not just in her imagination. "How do you do?" She held out a hand to Vivian.

Vivian stared at her, then at Franklin. Ever so slowly, her lip curled. "Mrs. *What*?"

Franklin blew out a breath. Corva had the impression that if he wasn't holding her arm with one of his and his cane in his other hand, he would have rubbed his face, possibly to hide.

"Corva and I have just been married," he said, offering no other explanation.

Vivian's transformation was quick and alarming. Her pretty smile evaporated into a sour grimace, which morphed into a bitter pout. "But Franklin," she choked. "*I* wanted to marry you."

The comment was so bold and had so much insistence behind it that Corva's brow shot up and her heart pounded against her ribs. Clearly, Vivian was a force to be reckoned with. Corva wanted to let Franklin's arm go and step away, possibly even running back to the train station, although the train had moved on.

"Vivian, you know what I've said about that in the past." Franklin kept his voice low and his eyes fixed on Vivian, almost as if he was scolding her.

"You said you would never marry anyone, that no one deserved a cripple for a husband," Vivian pouted.

Corva snuck a sideways glance to Franklin, who looked a little like a moth that had been skewered with a pin in a case. The same feeling of heartache that she'd sensed the moment she saw him returned.

Vivian turned her vicious stare on Corva and went on with her outburst. "I see now that you *lied*." Her chin and nose shot up. "I had no idea you were such a liar, Franklin Haskell. Papa will be furious."

"I'm sorry if you had the wrong idea about things." Franklin did his best to placate her. "I thought I had made my intentions clear from the first."

Vivian sniffed. "You didn't know what you were talking about. You were supposed to come around...eventually."

"You know that wasn't—" He stopped, pressing his lips together and squeezing his eyes shut.

It dawned on Corva that her new husband was a patient man. That thought made her smile, in spite of the confrontation they were mired in.

At last, Franklin took a breath, hugging his arm—and with it, Corva's hand—closer to his body. "I'm sorry if you are disappointed, Vivian, but with so many single men in these parts, I'm sure you'll find a husband in no time."

"Not one as rich—I mean, as refined as you," Vivian pouted.

"You never know." That was all the answer Franklin was going to give her, which made Corva proud. "If you will excuse us, I'm going to take Corva home now."

Vivian balled her fists at her sides and barely managed to swallow a frustrated growl. "Good day to you, then," she spit out. "And welcome to Haskell, Mrs. Haskell." She snorted. "That sounds so stupid."

As Vivian stomped off, heading back to the benches where the three women Corva assumed were her sisters sat, Franklin led Corva on.

"Sorry about that," he sighed. "I promise, I never gave Vivian any call to think she had hope where I am concerned. She won't be a problem."

"It's all right." Corva squeezed his arm. "I've known women like that before."

"I'm sorry for that too." The corner of Franklin's mouth twitched up.

A hope-filled chuckle bubbled through Corva's chest. Just as quickly, it flattened. Yes, she *had* known women like Vivian, which meant she knew she had to tread carefully around her going forward.

Chapter Three

Franklin couldn't decide if the day was going well or if it was a disaster. He refused to admit to himself that he'd worried Corva would take one look at him—one look at his braces—and get back on the train. But she hadn't. In fact, her reaction had set off waves of sparks in his gut. She'd thanked him, thanked him for marrying her. Guilt for every time in the last few weeks that he had come close to changing his mind and marching over to Aunt Ginny's house to call the whole thing off joined the mountain of guilt that already rested on his shoulders.

And yet, there Corva was, sitting next to him on the bench of his wagon, hands gripping the padded edge as she gazed in wonder at the mountains and plains around them. She was pretty, with a sweet, heart-shaped face and rosy lips. Her hair was a soft color—somewhere between light brown and blonde—with a hint of curl in its wispy ends. She was slight enough that a stiff wind could blow her over, but Franklin also got the sense she was as strong as an oak.

He cleared his throat to snag her attention as they passed through the wrought-iron archway marking the entrance of the ranch. "This is where my father's property starts."

Corva dragged her smile away from the blue sky of the mountainous horizon. "It's simply stunning here," she said in her lilting accent. "Truly paradise."

Franklin nodded, tempted to rub at the itching spot on his chest, right over his heart. "It was originally called Green Stream Ranch."

"Oh, no. Paradise Ranch suits it much better," she said before he could say pretty much the same thing.

"It's technically two ranches," he went on. "My father and his closest friend, Cyrus Piedmont, came out here more than twenty years ago and staked this claim, so to speak. They saw the potential in the land and brought in herds of the finest cattle well before most people saw that this was good ranch land."

"Did they have trouble with Indians?"

The flicker of worry in Corva's expression dredged up a wave of protectiveness that knocked Franklin off balance. As if he could truly protect her if it came down to it.

He shook his head in answer and to clear it. "Not particularly. Some. As much as anyone else. Dad has always been generous and helpful with the tribes in this area. Plus, Dr. Dean Meyers and Aiden Murphy—some of Haskell's most prominent citizens—work in close connection with both the Indians and the government. Aiden is the area Indian Agent."

"I see."

"When Cyrus Piedmont married my Aunt Virginia, Dad's sister," Franklin continued with the family history, "Dad gave them half the ranch as a wedding present."

"What a lovely gesture."

"It was." Franklin's expression pinched for a

moment. Old, bad memories rose up through his spine, as if the pain of his injuries were fresh again. "After Uncle Cyrus died and Mother moved back East for a time, there was some bad blood between Dad and Aunt Ginny for a while, a dispute over the property line."

"I take it things were solved?"

"Yes." It was all the answer he could give. How was he supposed to explain that his arrogant foolishness had been instrumental to the solution? Yes, the sins of his past may have helped his father and aunt to reconcile, but the very thought of the obnoxious braggart he had been back then turned his stomach.

"That's Aunt Virginia's house over that way." He pushed away the ache of those memories and the corresponding dull throb that was always present in his legs by pointing off to the left.

"That cluster of buildings there?" Corva sat straighter, raising a hand to shield her eyes as she looked. She leaned closer to him. The whiff of flowers came with her.

Franklin resisted the urge to scoot closer to her and breathe her in. "Yes. The biggest building is, of course, the barn, but that one off to the side, the large log house, is Aunt Ginny's house."

"What about the other, smaller ones?" Corva lowered her arm, looking to him for an explanation instead of off in the distance.

"One of them is a bunkhouse for Aunt Ginny's ranch hands. She employs about eight men to work her herd." He cleared his throat. "The other one is where her foreman, Jarvis Flint, and his family live."

He left it at that. There wasn't more he comfortable thinking about, let alone explaining. His arrogance all those years ago had manifested itself in clumsy attempts to court Alice, who was now Jarvis's wife. Hot shame painted his face at the thought.

"Over that way is Dad and Mother's house." He switched is reins to his other hand and pointed with his right arm across Corva's body. The gesture brought them into even closer contact. He pulled his arm back as if he'd reached too close to a fire.

Corva turned and shielded her eyes again to take a look at the other half of the ranch. "I see another big building, a barn?" Franklin hummed to tell her she was right. "And that must be a bunkhouse too, and a big house. Your father's house?"

"Mmm hmm."

They reached a narrow, dirt lane that forked away from the main road. Franklin steered his horse to take the wagon off the main drive.

Corva blinked in surprise. "We're not going to your father's house?"

"I don't live there." It was the simplest answer Franklin could give.

"Where do you live?"

Franklin nodded ahead, down the road. "I had this house built out by the stream. It's a pretty spot, and it's quiet."

"Oh." Corva leaned against the back of the bench. It was hard to tell if she liked the idea of living apart from everyone else or not.

Franklin covered the awkwardness of the moment by saying, "Dad has his own team of ranch hands. Technically I'm the head of that team, but with my legs, since I can't do any of the physical work involved in raising and herding cattle, I put a lot of trust in Travis Montrose."

"I see." Corva twisted to glance around him at his father's ranch as it faded into the distance.

"Travis came out here with his brothers, Mason and Cody, two years ago." It was strange to give an account of someone else's life, but he wasn't entirely sure how to handle his own at the moment. "Their parents had a farm and a ranch of some sorts way up in Oregon, but it failed when their father passed on about five years ago. Luckily, that was about the time Dad was advertising for more ranch hands, and since their ma was living with their sister at that point, all three of the brothers came down here."

"Interesting."

Franklin couldn't tell if it was interesting or not, but it was kind of Corva to at least pretend to be interested in what he was saying. It'd been so long since he'd had this much to say that he'd forgotten what it was like to carry on a conversation.

"Dad's baseball team is Howard's Hawks, by the way, and Aunt Virginia's is the Piedmont Panthers."

Corva brightened, her smile rivaling the sun. "How fun. Do you—" Instantly, her smile faded and she blushed. "No, I suppose not."

"I don't play," he confirmed her swallowed question. How many times had he sat in the benches watching a game, teeth clenched, longing to swing the bat and run? He cleared his throat and said, "The Hawks are playing the Bears on Sunday. That's why you saw the Bears practicing. Tomorrow, it's the Hawk's turn to practice on the field, although you can bet that Mason will have the boys throwing balls around and sprinting after work tonight. Mason is our team captain."

"I see," Corva answered, and again Franklin wondered if he was boring her.

That worry was short-lived. "We're here."

They crossed a wide, wooden bridge over a winding stream lined with shrubs and trees, and turned a corner. His modest house and stable came into view. Corva caught her breath and hummed.

"You'd hardly know this house was here from the other side of the stream," she said.

"I planned it that way," Franklin answered.

She turned to him, her eyes asking why, but he pretended not to see. Instead, he drove the wagon to stop beside a raised platform. The horse came to rest at just the right spot and bobbed his head with a snort as if to say, "We're home."

The platform was designed with a long ramp, so that all Franklin had to do was stand, take up his cane, and step carefully from the vehicle. Gideon Faraday—a scientist and inventor and another of Haskell's unique inhabitants, who also happened to be his brother-in-law— had built the ramp and another just like it leading up to Franklin's front door. In fact, after Gideon had gotten through altering the original house Franklin had built, there wasn't a single thing that Franklin had trouble climbing or reaching or doing with his broken legs.

Franklin was still slow to walk around the wagon, and by the time he made it to the other side, Corva had already hopped down on her own.

"Oh, sorry," she said when she saw his frown. "I should have waited for you to help me."

Franklin shook his head and waved as if it didn't matter, though somehow, deep in his heart, it did. Some husband he made. "Your weight probably would have knocked me over anyhow."

He was already halfway to forgetting the comment when Corva's face fell and she lowered her head. Franklin frowned, running back through his words. He wasn't saying that she was clumsy or heavy or anything. It was best to let it go and move on.

"Let me just get Kingsman settled here, and I'll show you the house."

Corva waited as patiently as she could while Franklin unhitched his horse from the wagon and led it into the simple stable. The first sight of her fiancé—no, her husband now—had raised a hundred questions about how he could navigate his way through the tasks of everyday life with iron braces on his legs. Walking was difficult enough. But as soon as he pulled the wagon up to the strange ramp in front of his stable, as soon as she saw a similar ramp leading to the front door of his house and caught a glimpse of other adjustments and contraptions inside the stable—like railings around the walls and a long stick with a claw on the end that must have been for reaching things on high shelves—she was fascinated.

So fascinated, that by the time Franklin finished settling his horse and limped slowly back to where she stood, she burst out with, "Franklin, were you born lame or did something happen?"

Franklin froze halfway through offering her his arm. He lowered his arm and glanced off toward the stream, face pinched.

Shame hit Corva like a lightning bolt. "I'm so sorry. I didn't mean to pry. It isn't my place."

Franklin took in a breath and offered his arm, escorting her on to the house. "I suppose if you look at it one way, it is your business now. You're my wife." He lowered his voice to a near whisper for the last statement.

Uncertainty crashed over Corva before she could stop it. Franklin didn't seem as overjoyed to be married as his

Aunt Ginny and Josephine did. He hadn't smiled once since she'd stepped off the train. His expression was strained now, and though it could have been pain from his legs, it could also have been dissatisfaction with the situation. Mrs. Breashears had mentioned that Virginia and Josephine and Mr. Charlie Garrett were interested in bringing brides out to Haskell, Wyoming, but she'd never actually said that Franklin Haskell was eager to be married. What if this whole thing was someone else's idea and she was an imposition?

All those thoughts zipped through her head in the time it took for Franklin to escort her around the parked wagon. "I had an accident about ten years ago," he began, then paused. "No, eleven years ago." He let out a breath and shook his head.

"I'm sorry," Corva murmured. She was, especially for her presence and for marrying him if that wasn't what he wanted.

"It was my own fault," he went on, staring at the ground in front of him. "I was young and arrogant and stupid. I..." He stopped, shook his head, then straightened his shoulders and looked her in the eye. "It was back when Dad and Aunt Ginny were bickering about the property line. There was a contest to build fences. Whoever finished their fence first got to claim the line was where they wanted it to be. I...I was brash and full of myself, and I tried to cheat by sabotaging the other side. Only, in the process, I upset a wagon full of heavy fence rails, and the whole thing came crashing down on me. By God's grace alone, none of the rails crushed my head or my vital organs. My legs, on the other hand... The lacerations alone nearly killed me, not to mention the breaks."

He let out a long breath and kept walking. It was almost as if the weight of those fence rails was still pressing down on him. Corva bit her lip. Poor Franklin still carried that burden, and now there was a distinct possibility he'd been burdened with a wife he didn't want either. He'd been kind and welcoming to her, but she couldn't say he'd been warm.

"I know how it feels to break a leg," she said after a respectful pause. Maybe he hadn't wanted her, but they were married now, and she was determined to be helpful to him and not another problem.

"You do?" He sounded far more surprised than she thought her revelation warranted.

"Mmm hmm." She tried to smile, but the terror of those memories turned it into something more like a grimace. "When I was a girl. We lived in Atlanta, Mama, Papa, and I. When the war started, Papa joined the cause, of course, so then it was just me and Mama. Then Sherman came."

A shudder passed through her. Franklin stopped at the bottom of the ramp leading up to his door, squeezing her arm.

Corva gathered her courage and said, "He burned Atlanta, you know."

"Yes, I'd heard."

"We were caught in the middle of it." She licked her lips as though she could still taste the ash and cinders. "They'd been telling us to evacuate for weeks, but Mama refused until the very end. We ran with only the few things we could carry. It was chaos—the fire, the gunshots, the animals and people dying. We made it to the edge of the city, but the crush of people was tremendous. I was only seven, and beside myself with fear. Mama tried to pull me out of the way of a burning carriage as it tore down the street, but she wasn't fast enough. It struck me. There was fire all around—pieces of the carriage, the collapsed building I fell near, my dress as it caught fire. It seemed like hours of nothing but flames and pain before Mama and a pair of soldiers pulled me free, though I'm told it was less than a minute. I'm lucky that only my leg was broken."

Franklin's expression twisted. Whatever emotion was rolling around behind those blue eyes of his, Corva couldn't decipher it. He continued to hold her arm, almost uncomfortably tight.

At last, he cleared his throat and said, "I'm sorry you had to go through that," in a rough voice.

Corva shrugged, and they continued on up the ramp to the narrow front porch. "That was a long time ago. As soon as I was pulled out of the burning debris, everyone around us came to our rescue instead of pushing and shoving. Mama got me to a doctor—I don't remember how—and he set the bone and treated my burns. I healed, and that was that." At least for the physical scars of the war. There were other scars Corva knew would never heal.

"What did your father say when he found out you were hurt?" They stopped at the top of the ramp.

Corva lowered her head, a lump forming in her throat. "We found out more than a month later that Papa had been killed in the Battle of Cedar Creek."

There was nothing else to be said. Part of Corva wanted to laugh at the gloom of one of the first personal conversations with her husband. It certainly wasn't the wedding day she had dreamed about as a girl.

Franklin hummed as though he shared her feeling that enough seriousness was enough. He turned to lead her on to the door.

They paused at the sight of the two tall, thin crates that held her paintings, her carpet bag, and paintbox.

"It looks like Luke beat us out here," Franklin said.

"How did he get here so fast?"

The corner of Franklin's mouth twitched as he peeked at her. "Luke is something of a daredevil. Whether it's wagons or horseback, liquor or women, he doesn't know the meaning of a moderate pace. He drives his ma, Josephine, to distraction."

Corva giggled, pressing her fingers to her lips. "Oh dear."

"I don't suppose you want these outside in the elements for too long." Franklin let go of her arm, took hold of the railing at the edge of the porch, and walked across to the crates. He inspected one, nudged it as if judging its weight, then turned back to open the front door.

"Do you mind if I go in and find a place for these?" Corva crossed to pick up her carpet bag and paint box.

"No, no, go right ahead." Franklin held his arm out, inviting her into his home.

Corva nodded, then stepped over the threshold. She smiled broadly at the sight of the room she walked into. Franklin was a single man who had been living by himself for a long time, or so she gathered, so his house could have been a disaster. Instead, it was tidy and organized. The front room was a combination parlor and dining room, with a stuffed sofa against one wall near a modest fireplace, and a polished dining table with four chairs close to the other wall. She caught a glimpse of a kitchen through a doorway beyond the dining area, and a bedroom through an open door on the side with the sofa. Another, closed door sat in the wall facing her. With a carpet on the floor that looked Turkish and ornate lamps on the dining table and a pair of side tables, the only thing that felt unfinished or rough about the space was the scarcity of decoration, particularly on the blank walls.

Corva drew in a breath, letting it out along with a good deal of her tension. Once again, her feelings about the unique situation she found herself in changed. Franklin may not have wanted a wife, but he had certainly picked the right one, at least if he wanted pictures on his walls.

She turned back to the door only to find Franklin struggling with one of her crates.

"Let me help with that." She dashed to the side to set her bag and paint box on the dining table, then met Franklin in the doorway.

"It's not particularly heavy," he grunted, shifting the crate. "One thing I can do around the ranch is lift things, as long as I'm stable, but I can't seem to balance this enough to lift it."

One peek at the frustration lining Franklin's face as he attempted to drag the crate into the doorway was enough to tell Corva not to comment on his struggle. "Maybe if I squeeze through and push from the other side."

She turned sideways and slid through the door beside Franklin. For one heightened moment, their bodies brushed against each other. Corva rested her hand against his shoulder to balance herself, more due to the dizziness of being so close to him. Struggles or not, she could feel the firmness of his chest and arms, the tautness of his stomach, as she slipped by him. Crippled legs or not, he was a man who kept himself in prime physical condition. Lifting things indeed.

By the time she stepped out onto the porch, her heart was pounding so fast even Luke would approve. She pressed a hand to her hot cheek to cool it, even though the gesture was far too obvious. Something else. She needed to think of something else before the awkwardness—was that awkwardness or was it...more?—consumed her. Franklin hadn't moved a muscle since the moment of contact.

When Corva finally dared to glance up at him, she found him studying her with more enigmatic and unreadable emotion in his eyes. That only made her flush deeper. He couldn't possibly—

"Whoa, whoa, I can help with that."

Both Corva and Franklin flinched and gasped at the interrupting voice. Corva twisted to see a tall, handsome man with long, dark blond hair tied at the base of his neck dismounting an equally handsome roan horse. He let the horse go with a pat to its flank, then strode toward the porch with long strides.

"Here," he said as he reached the doorway and the crates.

Franklin stepped back, lifting his hands in a gesture that almost looked like surrender. He backed into the house. Corva followed him. Seconds later, the long-haired man carried both of the crates inside as if they were nothing.

"Thanks, Jarvis." Franklin nodded for him to set the crates against the wall near the door.

"Don't mention it." Once his hands were free, Jarvis planted them on his hips and turned to where Franklin and Corva stood, side-by-side, a grin on his sun-touched face. "Is this the bride we've been hearing so much about?"

Franklin cleared his throat and sent Corva an apologetic smile. "Corva, I'd like you to meet Jarvis Flint."

The name rang a bell. "Oh. You're the one who works for Virginia Piedmont."

"I'm her foreman, you're right." Jarvis extended a hand.

Corva took it, impressed by how large and warm it was and how firm his handshake.

"It's a true honor to meet you, ma'am," he said, then, with a glance to Franklin, "We're all so happy that Franklin has finally found someone to settle down with."

Somewhere under the pleasantries, Corva caught a distinct feeling that he was also implying "We've all been worried about him."

"I'm happy to be here," Corva answered. She glanced to Franklin, making sure he knew her comment was as much for him as for Jarvis.

An awkward pause followed. Corva waited for Franklin to say something, but his lips seemed to be glued shut, and a flush had come to his cheeks. Without touching him, she could see his muscles had gone hard as rocks. Jarvis seemed equally as much at a loss for words and ground his toe into the carpet. The silence between the two men was as good as a novel.

"Anyhow." Jarvis finally broke the silence, as if they were in the middle of a conversation instead of stuck in a ditch beside one. He shifted his weight and let his hands drop. "I came to talk to you about the calves."

Business took over, and Franklin transformed before Corva's eyes. He stood straighter, squared his shoulders, and frowned. "What about them?"

"Some are missing," Jarvis said. "Well, I guess that's what you call it when a cow goes out to pasture plump and pregnant and comes back not pregnant." He glanced to Corva. "If you'll pardon my saying, ma'am."

"It's fine." Corva waved away the frank talk.

"They're coming back not pregnant?" Franklin

crossed his arms, rubbing his chin. "And no calves with them?"

"None."

"How many?" Franklin asked.

"At least half a dozen in the last week," Jarvis answered.

Franklin arched an eyebrow. "Has anyone gone to check how many calves Bonneville has in his herd at the moment?"

At the question, the air in the room went alive with an electric charge. Anxious prickles made their way down Corva's back. "Are you suggesting Mr. Bonneville might have somehow taken the calves right out of their mothers?" The idea seemed ridiculous and abhorrent to her.

Jarvis shrugged and grimaced. "Not exactly taking them out, but watching to see as soon as they're born, then whisking them off and pretending they're part of his herd."

"You see, there's a lot of open range around here," Franklin went on to explain. "Everyone brands their cattle so that we can tell them apart, but calves who are born out on the range aren't branded. If someone were to snatch one and whisk it away, out of sight, they could claim that it was from their herd all along and brand it before anyone can protest."

"Isn't that cheating?" Corva asked.

It was the wrong thing to say. Franklin flushed and glanced away, almost as if he wished he was somewhere else. Jarvis squirmed as though someone had dropped a worm down the back of his shirt. Both men suddenly looked as though they would rather be on different continents, let alone in the same room.

One blink, and Corva knew why. The story Franklin

had told her about the fence-building competition, about how he had tried to cheat and ended up with crushed legs. She didn't need to ask to know that Jarvis was involved in that, probably deeply involved.

She bit her lip, remembering the promise she'd made to herself to be helpful to Franklin instead of causing him more problems. "What do you plan to do? How can you prove what Mr. Bonneville has done, or even that it's him?"

Slowly, both men shook themselves out of whatever attack of awkwardness they'd fallen prey to.

"Bonneville has pulled stunts like this before," Jarvis explained. "He wants to be at the top of the totem pole in these parts."

"A position my father will not let go of lightly," Franklin added. "He won't take rustling like this lightly either."

"Exactly." Jarvis nodded. "The problem is, how do we approach Bonneville about the possible thefts without setting him off on another one of his tears?"

Corva breathed an inner sigh of relief. The two men were back to discussing business.

Franklin sighed and rubbed his forehead. "We've barely settled from the last dust-up."

"With Mr. Bonneville?" Corva asked.

Jarvis grunted. "Rex Bonneville is a thorn in all of our sides. The trouble is, he's a member of the Wyoming Stock Grower's Association."

"Dad joined too, earlier this year," Franklin put in.

"But he doesn't make the trips out to Cheyenne to socialize with the other ranch owners the way Bonneville does."

Franklin grunted. "That's half the problem right there, if you ask me. Bonneville is more interested in cards and cigars and more with that lot than with overseeing his business."

Feeling one step behind, Corva asked, "What's the Wyoming Stock Grower's Association?"

"It's a group here in Wyoming that oversees standards and practices of Wyoming ranchers and the open range," Jarvis explained. "It was formed a couple of years ago, but already, its members control just about everything in the state, making the elected government seem like a puppet show."

"Dad may control just about every aspect of Haskell as its founder and mayor," Franklin added, "But Bonneville keeps threatening to call in his big guns to bring him down."

"It sounds like a delicate dance," Corva said.

"It's something, all right," Jarvis grumbled. He took a breath, shifted his weight, and said, "Well, I just wanted to find you to make sure you knew about that."

"Thanks. I appreciate it," Franklin answered.

Jarvis nodded, then smiled at Corva. "I'll leave the two of you to get better acquainted."

He nodded once more, then turned to go. Then it was just the two of them again.

"I...I suppose I need to unpack my things and get settled." Corva moved toward the table where she'd left her carpetbag. "I don't have much."

Franklin crossed the main room to the open bedroom door. "I've had the guest room made up for you. I hope you like it."

Corva paused halfway through turning around, a lump in her throat. "The guest room?"

Franklin scratched the back of his neck, wincing for a moment before meeting her eyes. "I figured it was too soon for us to share a room. Since we just met and all."

How thoughtful of him…and how uncomfortable. It was as clear as day that he wasn't ready for a real marriage.

Corva forced her back to relax and put on a smile anyhow. There would be time for all that later. "Thank you," she said, carrying her bag across the room to the spare bedroom. "It's lovely."

Once again, they ended up standing closer to each other than was strictly proper as Corva crossed through the doorway. Instead of feeling threatened or endangered, as she had far too many times before in similar situations, Corva felt safe. If that wasn't a good sign of things to come, she didn't know what was.

The differences between Nashville and Paradise Ranch became astoundingly apparent to Corva early the next morning as she woke from a heavy sleep. Living at Hurst Home—and before that at her uncle's house—waking was always accompanied by the bustle of traffic outside, of early morning hawkers out selling their wares, and, on good mornings, the rich baritone of the cobbler's assistant as he walked to work, singing old plantation songs.

The only songs Wyoming held were the twitter of birds greeting the dawn, the call of a hawk somewhere in the distance, and the brush of trees swaying in a breeze. A beam of sunlight slanted through a crack in the guestroom curtain, spilling across the bed where Corva lay under a thick quilt, perfect for nights that were still chilly. The whole thing was so serene that she closed her eyes again, feeling that, for once, she was completely safe.

She awoke a second time to the clatter of pots in the kitchen.

"Blast." A crack of fear burst through her, and with it, memories of at least a hundred blows and insults.

Gasping, Corva launched herself out of bed and scrambled into clean clothes. The few things she had were old and wrinkled after spending the last week in her carpetbag during the journey. She was sure she looked like a destitute waif as she rushed out of the guest room and through the main room to the kitchen, but it was better to fix breakfast looking like a drudge and have it hot on the table by the time her uncle woke up than to feel the back of his—

She stopped in the kitchen doorway, and slapped a hand to her pounding heart. No, she wasn't in Nashville anymore. Franklin wasn't Uncle Stanley. That was all behind her, hundreds of miles away. Still, it was rude of her to sleep in.

Franklin was stationed at the stove, leaning against a contraption that looked like a cane with a leather seat on top, frying bacon. The legs of his trousers hung loose, no braces in sight.

"I'm sorry." She scurried up to the counter where a loaf of bread and a knife stood waiting. "I shouldn't have slept in. It was irresponsible of me, unforgivable. I promise never to let it happen again." Her hands shook as she picked up the knife.

It wasn't until she had sliced four pieces and slid them into the toasting rack on the stovetop that she realized Franklin was staring at her. She dragged her eyes to meet his, expecting to see anger, or at the very lease disapproval.

He watched her with nothing more than surprise. And perhaps a shade of bewilderment.

"I figured you were tired after such a long journey and would want to sleep in," he said, soft and simple. "I make breakfast every day, so it's no skin off my back."

"Oh. I'm sorry." Corva turned away, reaching for a

bowl of eggs. "I...I was always the one to make breakfast at home." The truth was more like her uncle insisted she wake up at the crack of dawn to have a full breakfast waiting for him when he rolled out of bed, but it sounded much nicer the way she said it.

Franklin saw beyond her words. "You cooked such a magnificent supper last night. I don't mind cooking breakfast. I'm an early riser anyhow, and generally need to be over at the paddock beside Dad's house when the other ranch hands get there."

"I don't mind, really."

He paused, continuing to study her, then said, "Hurst Home is a place where women go when they've come out of some sort of dangerous predicament."

Corva lowered her eyes.

Another pause, and Franklin said, "I may not be good for much, but I know how to treat a woman...and how not to treat her."

Tears clogged Corva's eyes and squeezed her throat. A younger version of herself would never have dreamed of a man saying that to her, and here Franklin was, making a dream come true without her having to explain what it was. He deserved at least a smile for that.

She took in a breath, stood straighter, and smiled with all the gratitude of her heart. "Thank you." That was all she needed to close the door on her past and focus on the first breakfast she would cook because she wanted to in years. She nodded to the skillet of bacon. "That looks just about ready. Do you usually make your eggs in the same pan with the bacon fat, or do you use a fresh pan?"

"With the bacon fat, of course." The tension around Franklin's eyes and mouth dissolved. It was his version of a smile. "Everything is better with bacon."

The rest of breakfast went more smoothly than Corva

could ever have imagined. Franklin knew his way around a kitchen, but he also knew how to carry on a conversation across a table. As they ate and drank tea—Franklin preferred it over coffee, and Corva was happy for one more, tiny difference from her uncle's ways—he explained the various gadgets around his house that made his life easier.

"The stick I was using in the kitchen is one of the few things that Gideon Faraday didn't invent and make especially for me. It's called a shooting stick, and is used in England by aristocrats outdoors on hunts. Very handy for taking unnecessary strain off of your legs."

"I can imagine."

He paused, swirled his fork through the remaining yolk on his plate, then said, "I'm not helpless. After the accident, it felt like everyone I knew saw it as their responsibility to take care of me, to do everything for me. Aside from the fact that I didn't and don't deserve that kind of attention, I hated feeling like a useless lump and an overgrown child."

Corva focused on his eyes, trying to read what he was really saying. "I wouldn't dream of treating you that way," she ventured. "But as your wife, it's my responsibility to share the load."

Franklin tipped his head to the side. "True. I'm sure, given time, we'll figure out our way around each other." He planted his hands on the table and pushed himself to a standing position.

Corva's smile faltered. She had no idea what to make of her unusual, new husband. Were his words a promise to form a true union or was he putting her off somehow? She stood as well, taking her plate and his into the kitchen to wash.

No. She shook her head to clear it. This marriage

would never work if she constantly walked on eggshells, expecting Franklin to treat her the way her uncle had. Her worth in her husband's eyes would not depend on how fast she worked or how efficiently she evaded his notice. Wyoming was a new world and Paradise Ranch a new life. She had a chance of being appreciated for who she was here.

"I'll come home for lunch," Franklin called from the other room. "Generally, I stay over at Dad's and eat with the other ranch hands."

Corva set the plates in the sink, under soapy water, then strode to the door. "You don't need to change your plans for me."

She stopped at the sight of Franklin sitting on the sofa, strapping his braces to his legs. One brace was propped against the sofa beside him. Open as it was, it reminded her too much of an iron cage, a prison that he willfully closed himself in. True, he could barely walk at all without them, but something about the cold, claw-like metal sent a chill down her back.

"I don't mind coming back here," Franklin went on, unaware of her thoughts. "To tell you the truth, I don't much like sitting down with the ranch hands."

Corva's brow flew up. "Really? Why?" Was it possible that he didn't think he had a right to be with them? That he wasn't man enough?

"I'm their boss," he said, reaching for the other brace and securing it around his leg. "Not only that, I'm younger than half of them. It makes for some awkward conversations."

"Oh." Yes, she suppose that made sense too. "I'll make sure to have a hearty meal ready for you by, well, would noon be good?"

"You don't have to—" He stopped, his hands pausing

over the buckles on his braces, and let out a breath, relaxing. "Noon would be fine." The corners of his mouth twitched.

What she wouldn't do to coax a smile out of her husband.

When he stood, braces in place, and walked across the room to fetch his cane from its spot near the door, his movements were clunky, but faster than without the braces. Corva waited in the kitchen doorway, wondering if he would come over to kiss her goodbye.

"I'll be off now," he said instead, nodded, then headed out.

As soon as the door clicked shut behind him, Corva's heart began to race. It was the opposite reaction from what she should have, but there she was, alone in a house she had yet to feel was her home.

She drew in a breath and took a look around, studying the space without Franklin in it. It really was a delightful house. The walls were straight and covered with wallpaper bearing a subtle, geometric design. The fireplace in the main room was well-maintained and clean. The furniture was neat and artfully arranged. What surprised her the most was that she hadn't noticed the details of the place while Franklin was there. Her husband somehow demanded all of the attention in the room without raising his voice or stomping around. Corva hummed to herself as that thought struck her. Yes, she could be happy here, and she might just stand a chance of pleasing Franklin too.

The first order of business in gaining her new husband's approval was to clean up breakfast. If Franklin was the sort to keep his space clean on his own, she would keep it doubly clean while she was there. She scrubbed and put away the breakfast dishes, cleaned the counters and the stove, then mopped the floor for good measure. Each chore was something she'd done daily before, but now she actually took pride in her work, hoping it would provide a good impression instead of fearing it would earn her more bruises.

Once the kitchen was taken care of, she moved on to tidying the main room and the bedrooms. Franklin's bedroom was his own, private space, so she only gave it a quick dusting and smoothed out the already-made bed, giving herself a few seconds to wonder about the rails and other inventions the room contained to make his life easier.

The real fun came when she finished with the cleaning and opened her crates. Her heart leapt with joy as she cracked open first one, then the other, and slid out the paintings that had been her only friends for so many years. She spread them around the room, propping them against the table, the sofa, and the walls, saying hello.

She spent a good half hour shuffling the paintings from one spot to another. Some were portraits—her mother, her father, and one of the maid who had lived across the street from her uncle's house who had been her friend. A few were cityscapes. Most, however, were landscapes. Nothing made Corva happier than painting sunlight in the trees or dewdrops on grass.

The last item she unpacked from the crates was her beloved easel. Any other artist would probably scoff at the collection of patched and glued sticks that was Corva's easel. Her mother had bought it for her new and whole when she was young, but as soon as her uncle had caught on to just how much Corva loved it, loved painting, he had taken out his rage by smashing the fragile frame and breaking it to splintered pieces. There was nothing Corva could do to purchase a new one, so each time it was broken, she would lovingly patch it back together, fixing the pieces in place with glue, wrapping them with strips of muslin, and doing whatever it took to get it on its feet. Now it stood crooked, and it wobbled if she put her weight against it wrong, but she wouldn't have traded it for the world.

She couldn't resist taking it straight outside, out into the panorama of amazing views that surrounded the house. The problem now was not so much what she should paint, it was which majestic vista she should start with. Forgetting all else, she chose a spot to the side of the house, facing the stream and a stand of sun-touched trees. One thing led to another, she rushed back into the house to fetch her paint box and the last blank canvas she owned, and a stool. She told herself she would only sketch out the painting, mark her spot so she could come back to it when she had more time, then go back inside to fix lunch.

Two hours later, with greens and browns and blues popping on the canvas as the scene took shape, Franklin came riding up the path.

"Oh, no," Corva gasped, putting her palate and brush down so fast she nearly threw them. "Lunch."

Her panic was cut short at the figure Franklin cut atop his horse. He still had his braces around his legs, but he sat so easily atop his horse that without those braces, there would be no way to tell what was wrong with him, if anything. His back was straight, and he moved as one with the horse. More than just competent, he looked dazzlingly handsome in the noon sunlight. Her heart flipped in her chest…and not from fear of her negligence.

"Oh good," he said as he rode closer. "You found something to do. I was afraid you'd spend all your time cooking and cleaning and getting bored."

She winced and rose from her stool, wringing her hands. "I'm afraid I got carried away and lost track of time. I'll get started on your lunch right away."

His only answer was a slight frown. Was he upset? Had she made him angry by getting distracted? Or was he just curious? A hundred possibilities flitted through her mind as he rode right up to her side, handling his horse with expert skill. From his seat high above, he glanced down at her new painting, then at the stretch of stream that was her model. Something dark and troubled settled over him.

"It's nice." He quickly turned his horse and marched off to the same ramp he'd used to climb down from the wagon the day before.

"Nice?" Corva murmured, too quiet for Franklin to hear. She peeked at her painting. He didn't like it. There could be no other explanation. He'd turned away so quickly. "Nice." She bit her lip and marched away, leaving her work where it was. It would be all right where it was until after lunch.

Franklin dismounted with the help of his ramp, and followed Corva into the house.

"I can fix you something for lunch from the leftovers you have on hand." Corva rushed ahead of him to the kitchen. "Your pantry is well-stocked."

Franklin didn't follow her into the kitchen. Through the kitchen doorway, she could see him studying her paintings. She'd hung most of them before going outside. As she rushed back and forth between the kitchen and the pantry, she couldn't get a clear view of his expression. Did he like her work, or did he think it was just "nice?" Suddenly, his opinion of her talent meant everything.

She tried not to dwell on it as she put together a plate

of cold chicken and some sort of leftover cold bean salad that had been in his icebox. She brought two plates to the table, but was far too agitated to sit.

"Are you sure it's all right for me to have hung them?" she asked, frustrated at the shake in her voice.

Franklin took his time replying. Every second that ticked by made Corva more anxious. Her husband was the most unreadable man she'd ever met. Not smiling was one thing, but not betraying an ounce of opinion one way or another in how he looked at things was near maddening.

At last, he said, "Since we're so far away from any city with an art gallery, these will do."

It was as if the air itself dropped flat to the floor, taking Corva's stomach with it. These would do? Her whole heart and soul, every stifled, tangled emotion she'd been forced to keep locked away lest she provoke her uncle's wrath, all her happiness for the past ten years on display for anyone to see...and it *would do*?

She couldn't speak. Throat tight with tears that she refused to shed, she fled into the kitchen to pour two glasses of water to go with lunch. Through the window, she caught sight of her easel and the new painting she had started. What was the point of starting another one if the best it could ever be was adequate?

Franklin was seated at the table when Corva returned and placed a glass of water at the top of his plate. "They found one of the calves this morning," he said as if he hadn't just brought her world down with a careless comment. "At least, we assume it's one of ours. Cody Montrose found it suckling one of our cows, but it had already been branded by Bonneville. It's shameless to brand a calf that young."

All Corva could manage in reply was a nod. She

hadn't been married for a full day yet, and already she despaired that she would never be truly accepted for who she was, no matter what place she found in Wyoming.

The calf that was found in Howard Haskell's herd bearing Rex Bonneville's brand was almost certainly one of Howard's. Franklin mulled over that truth and what it would mean for relations between the two ranches as he drove Corva over the short distance between his house and his parents'. It would be too easy for Bonneville to claim some sort of mistake or negligence on the part of one of his ranch hands, but it didn't explain the other missing calves. Bonneville wasn't the sort of man to confess to the crime and make amends. He wasn't the sort to go on the attack either, fortunately, or they could have an even bigger problem on their hands. Grazing cattle on the open range had already made for some dicey situations between competing ranchers.

A short cough from Corva on the bench beside him reminded Franklin that—for a change—he wasn't alone. He scolded himself for disappearing into himself to tackle the problems of the ranch instead of focusing on making her comfortable. She'd been so quiet since he'd come back from his day's work to announce that his parents were hosting a supper for them tonight at the big house. That must have been why she was so withdrawn.

"There really isn't much to worry about at my parents' house." He thought about reaching over to pat her knee to reassure her, but she was seated just a few inches too far away, hands clasped tightly in her lap. "And by that I mean that it will be loud, crowded, and overwhelming."

She snapped her head up to stare at him with wide eyes. Was she looking more pale than that morning?

His lips twitched into something close to a reassuring smile as he snuck a look at her. "So there's no sense in worrying when you know it'll be a madhouse."

"Oh." She lowered her head and stared at her hands once more.

Franklin frowned. He barely knew the pretty, quiet woman beside him—even though she was his wife—but instinct told him something was wrong. How could he have messed something so important up so quickly? What had he done?

He cleared his throat, scrambling to fix the situation. "My sister, Lucy, will be there with her husband, Gideon, and their children. All you need to do is get Lucy to like you—and my sister likes everyone—and she'll do all the talking for you all night."

Corva nodded, still staring at her hands, her lips stretched in a tight line that might have been an attempt at a smile.

Franklin clenched his jaw, stomach turning. What had happened? Things were so smooth this morning? They'd been fine at lunch too. Sure, Corva had forgotten to make lunch, but considering how blissful she'd looked while painting, he didn't mind at all. Judging by the beauty and brightness of the paintings she'd hung around his house—their house—painting was something she loved. She was brilliant at it too, good enough to have a gallery. That was far more important than lunch.

He had almost found the perfect words to tell her that, and to reassure her that he had no ill feelings about eating leftovers for lunch, when they arrived at his parents' house.

"Hey, Franklin," Cody Montrose called out to him. "Need some help?"

Franklin had long since stopped feeling insecure

when any of the Montrose brothers offered him a hand, or even when they all but picked him up and carried him, as Cody did when he lifted Franklin out of the wagon. Once Franklin's feet were on the ground, Cody backed off without a second look, as though carrying his boss around was normal, and Franklin proceeded around the wagon to help Corva down.

"I heard that Mrs. Evans and Mrs. Piedmont mailed off for a bride for you," Cody went on, studying Corva with mischief-filled eyes, "but I was certain she'd have buck teeth and a hump or something."

Franklin lifted Corva down from the wagon as Cody spoke. Their eyes met, and Franklin smirked, darting a look in Cody's direction. "He has an unfortunate tendency of speaking the first thing that comes to his mind," he confided, too quiet for Cody to hear. "It's usually not savory."

For a heartbeat, Corva grinned at him, genuinely amused. Her feet reached the ground, but neither of them let go. It felt right to hold her so close, as if he could banish whatever mistake he'd made earlier by holding her, and maybe kissing her.

A burst of muffled laughter from inside the house reminded Franklin that there were over a dozen people eager to meet Corva and fuss and tease him, and to make quiet moments of hugging and stillness impossible. He let Corva go, retrieved his cane with one hand, and tucked her hand into his elbow.

"She's actually pretty," Cody went on as the two of them reached his side. They headed to the porch and the ramp that had been built specifically for Franklin. "Maybe I should ask Mrs. Evans and Mrs. Piedmont to find a wife for me too. Isn't there an entire house of brides just waiting to come out here?"

"Hurst Home," Corva answered, her voice shaky at first. "I was living at Hurst Home in Nashville before I came here. I believe the owner, Mr. Charlie Garrett, lives in Haskell."

"I play cards with Charlie on occasion," Cody said. "Good fellow. Wicked at a card table, but good everywhere else."

They reached the front door, and, as if people had been lying in wait, it burst open.

"Here they are." Lucy stepped into the doorway—belly round with yet another child, arms spread wide. She pulled Corva into the house with a hug that knocked her off-balance. "At last, I have a sister. Thank God in heaven that Aunt Ginny was smart enough to send off for you to come. You have no idea how desperately my brother needs looking after. He's simply hopeless, always has been, and we've been terribly worried about him. But you're here now, and our worries are over. Come meet everyone."

Franklin had enough time to catch and squeeze Corva's hand and to say, "I should have warned you, she talks and no one can stop her," before Lucy whisked Corva off to the sofa, where the women were fawning over Alice Flint's newborn.

A flush of awkwardness threatened to close Franklin down. Corva next to Alice Flint. Alice, who he'd made such a fool of himself over all those years ago, who he'd been trying to impress when he climbed up on that wagon of fence rails and upset it.

"She seems nice." Travis Montrose stepped up to his side, slapping a hand on Franklin's back and keeping him from sinking into the mire of regrets that should have been long-buried.

"She is, so far," Franklin answered.

Luke Chance stepped up to his other side. "Congratulations, boss. But the real question is 'Can she cook?'"

Travis chuckled. Franklin's lips twitched close to a grin. "She made a mean breakfast. Well, we made it together."

"That's all a man needs." Luke nodded.

Franklin shook his head. "A man needs far more than a good cook."

"Right. There's *that* too." Luke winked.

Franklin heated and cleared his throat, turning to where Corva was now seated on the sofa beside Alice. She looked bewildered as the baby was handed into her arms. Franklin's ten-year old niece, Minnie, bounced by Corva's side, torn between giving her attention to the baby or her new aunt. Minnie never could sit still.

"Actually, it turns out that Corva is an amazing artist," he told Travis and Luke. "She brought a bunch of paintings with her, and they're astounding. I might suggest she talk to Mother about places she could display them."

"If she's really that good, she should talk to Mr. Kline at the mercantile about selling them," Mason Montrose suggested as he crossed behind Franklin on his way to the supper table. Franklin's brother-in-law, Gideon, nodded in agreement from several feet away and edged closer.

"She is that good," Franklin said, although maybe it wasn't the best idea to go talking about his new wife where anyone passing could eavesdrop.

"So what's this I hear about Rex Bonneville stealing newborn calves?" Gideon asked.

"I swear, the next time I see that man, I'm going to give him a black eye." Cody stepped over to join them.

All talk of Corva was forgotten as the men launched

into a heated discussion of rustling and strategies of how they could thwart Bonneville and expose his thievery. Franklin let the others take the lead in the conversation, listening in, but also keeping an eye on Corva. The baby had brightened her up considerably, and even though the men moved away from the front parlor where the women were gathered, he watched her greet the gaggle of children—his nieces and nephews, and Jarvis and Alice Flint's children—with relaxed friendliness. A hitch formed in Franklin's chest. He hadn't asked Corva outright if she wanted children of her own, but clearly she was good with them.

Children. Her children would be his children. What kind of father would he make? How would it be between them conceiving those children?

"Ladies and gentlemen, supper is served," Virginia announced from the hallway that divided the dining room from the front parlor. "Food's on the table, but you'll have to find a seat somewhere else, since there's too many of us to fit."

Chaos followed as family and ranch hands alike jostled to get to the dining room table first. It was something of a tradition to act like heathens when a banquet was being served in Howard Haskell's house.

"A little healthy competition is good for the soul," Howard declared—as usual—over the rush and noise and laughter that followed.

Franklin always hung back at these stampedes. With his braces and cane, there was no way he could muscle his way to the front of the pack, and as much as his father encouraged him to use his cane to beat away the competition, Franklin would rather end up with table scraps than raise a hand against anyone, even in jest.

"What's going on?" Corva whispered breathlessly,

squeezing close to his side as Minnie tore past, burrowing through the adults to get to the table.

Franklin looped his free arm around Corva's waist to shelter her from Mason as he carried his plate above his head back into the parlor, looking for a seat. "We have a tradition of chaos at the supper table in the Haskell house," he explained. "Hang back or you might be trampled."

He meant it as a joke, but Corva made a strangled noise, as though she took him at his word. "I've never seen anything like this," she whispered. "In my uncle's house, anyone who made any noise or pushed and shoved like this, besides him, would have seen the strap."

Her words were like a punch in his gut. He tightened his hold on her waist, peeking at her. The reflection of old fear in her eyes had him ready to forgo his pledge of non-violence. "Your uncle." He swallowed, not sure how to form the question that needed to be asked. "Was he…cruel?"

Corva tensed beside him, staring down at the floor. It was a clearer answer than her reply of, "This isn't the time to talk about it."

Anger burst through Franklin's chest. In its wake was an even stronger feeling of protectiveness. He knew that Corva had come from a sad background, but in that moment, he felt it too.

"What are you two doing just standing there?" Virginia pushed her way through everyone who was finished fixing their plates and had turned to looking for a seat instead. "There's still plenty of good cuts of meat, and far more vegetables than there should be." She turned to the hall. "Who isn't eating their vegetables?"

"Mr. Cody isn't," nine-year-old Christopher Flint hollered.

"Hush up, boy," Cody hollered back, all in fun. They both giggled.

"I don't think I'll ever fit in here," Corva sighed.

Franklin gave her waist one last squeeze, then escorted her to the end of the table where the plates were. "I've never fit in," he confessed, "but you do get used to it."

They made their way around the table, filling plates with everything from steak to peas to pasta. It was decidedly convenient to have Corva hold the plates while Franklin used his free hand to scoop delicacies onto them. Yet another way the two of them could work well together. Franklin planned to seat the two of them on the stairs in the hall—his usual spot. He should have known his father would have other ideas.

"No hiding away in the hall for you this time, Franklin, my son," he said in his booming voice. "Bring your pretty, new wife in here. We've reserved you a place of honor."

The place of honor turned out to be two chairs that had been set front and center before the fireplace. Franklin sent Corva a look of apology, then escorted her into the heart of the crush of enthusiastic family and friends. Corva had been pale before they arrived, but now she was flushed and wide-eyed.

"So Corva, tell us all about who you are," Howard asked once they were settled.

"Howard, hush," Franklin's mother, Elizabeth, swatted his arm. "Let the poor girl eat."

"Nonsense," Howard declared, his mouth half full of mashed potatoes. "She's my daughter-in-law now, and I want to know something about her. Where were you living before Hurst Home, for example?" He pointed a turkey drumstick at her.

"I..." Corva hesitated.

Franklin rested a hand on her arm. "You don't have to play along if you don't want to," he whispered. "I'll handle it."

She swallowed, then whispered back, "It's all right. He's your father." She cleared her throat, sat straighter, then said to Howard, "I have been living in Nashville for the past eight years, with...with my aunt and her husband, my...my Uncle Stanley." For a moment, she turned downright green.

The wave of protectiveness Franklin had felt before rushed through him again tenfold.

"What did your uncle do?" Howard asked on.

"Not much," Corva murmured, then answered, "He was an instructor at University of Nashville."

"What did he teach?" Elizabeth asked.

"Mathematics," Corva answered, her voice quieter.

"Why did he want to teach mathematics?" little Christopher asked, scrunching his face in a grimace.

"He likes things that are logical," Corva all but whispered.

Franklin had to put a stop to this line of questioning. Clearly, it upset Corva, and he wouldn't have that. "Dad, what are your plans for confronting Bonneville about the calves?"

Behind them, Cody laid a few more logs on the fire to brighten the room, as if it wasn't hot enough already in spite of the spring chill outside.

"Now, now, son." Howard shook a finger at him. "First things first. We're investigating...I mean, learning about your wife." He winked at Corva.

Corva blushed and stared down at her plate.

"Dad, maybe now isn't the best time," Franklin defended her.

"Nonsense. Now, young lady, what about your parents? Where are they?"

Corva swallowed. "My father was killed in the war. My mother died right after the war ended. That's when I was sent to live with my Aunt Mildred, because the family thought we would cheer each other up."

"Well? Did you?" Howard demanded.

Franklin cringed. He knew his father meant well, but he was like a grizzly bear in a house of cards. Franklin tried to shake his head to call his father off, but Howard was oblivious.

"No, not really," Corva answered. "Aunt Mildred didn't like children. She…she married my Uncle Stanley two years later, but…" She closed her mouth and swallowed.

Franklin saw the tell-tale signs of a woman about to cry. "Dad, I know you want to learn all about Corva, but this business with Bonneville is far more pressing. We need every one of those calves to stay with our herd if we stand a chance of increasing our numbers."

"The only solution I can think of is to keep the pregnant cows close to home," Travis spoke up.

Franklin sent him a nod of thanks.

Howard sighed. "I doubt Bonneville himself is behind it. More likely it's that bast—" He cleared his throat, darting a glance at the women and children present. "That scoundrel he's got running his operation, Brandon."

"Kyle Brandon is a menace," Travis growled.

A snap sounded from the fireplace behind Franklin and Corva. Franklin ignored it, but Corva turned, as if only just realizing she'd been seated in front of it. The logs Cody had laid on the fire had caught and now blazing away.

One look at the flames, and Corva screamed, launching out of her chair. Her plate spilled to the carpet. She only made it two steps before stumbling over one of the children.

Franklin thrust his plate aside and jumped up after her. "It's okay," he assured her, closing his arms around her and drawing her into an embrace, even though he wasn't all that steady himself. "It's okay."

Corva hid her face against his shoulder with a sob. She shook like a leaf, so Franklin tightened his hold around her. Throughout the room, his family and friends gaped and murmured in baffled surprise.

"She lived through the burning of Atlanta," he told them quietly.

A few hums and nods of sympathy followed, but Corva continued to shake and refused to come out of hiding.

"Move those chairs," Howard ordered, blustering, but red-faced with embarrassment. "What fool put them there in the first place?"

Probably him, but Franklin wasn't going to say anything.

"I'll fix you a new plate, dear," his mother said, patting Corva's back as she skipped through the room to the dining room.

"Why is Aunt Corva crying?" Minnie asked.

Everyone jumped into motion to drown the impertinence of Minnie's question, shuffling seats and moving Franklin and Corva's chairs to the hallway side of the parlor. There was so much movement and fuss that not one of them heard the front door open and slam shut.

It wasn't until he shouted, "Haskell, I demand you stop this underhanded farce at once," that they realized Rex Bonneville had barged into the house.

Chapter Five

Corva had never been so ashamed in her life. These people were her hosts, her in-laws, and she had lost her head over a measly fireplace. But turning to find fire where she hadn't expected there to be a blaze was too much. Still, that was no excuse to cause a scene. She didn't know what she would have done if Franklin hadn't jumped up to steady her. He was the perfect hiding place at the perfect time, only now she wasn't sure how she could show her face again with dignity.

"What is the meaning of this?" Howard Haskell, her new father-in-law bellowed.

Corva wanted to disappear into the floorboards, melt like paints left out in the rain. She sagged into Franklin, no idea how she could explain herself.

"You're asking me the meaning of this?" an unfamiliar voice boomed from somewhere behind Franklin's back. "I'm the one who came here for an answer. I will not have my good name sullied by madmen like you."

"Now see here—" Howard thundered.

"You have no right to march into a private

residence," Virginia barked at the same time.

Movement swirled around her, but it wasn't until Franklin pivoted to face the hall that Corva realized none of it concerned her. Slowly, cautiously, still shaking, she lifted her head from Franklin's shoulder.

Standing in the front of the hall near the door was a giant of a man with broad shoulders and a sweeping, grey overcoat. He had dark hair that was slicked back and a pointed beard and curling moustache. His expression was a mixture of fury and disgust. The picture he presented, high cheekbones, the line of his nose, his sneering disgust, struck an all-too familiar note of fear in Corva's gut.

"Get out, Bonneville."

As soon as Howard named him, Corva gasped. Rex Bonneville. So this was the man that Franklin had told her about, that everyone had been discussing. This was the calf thief.

"I'm not going anywhere until you answer for the libelous rumors you've been spreading." Bonneville crossed his arms, staring down his long nose at Howard. He was a good six inches taller than Franklin's father...than everyone.

A moment later, Corva noticed the two men standing on either side of Bonneville, slightly behind them. One was short but had muscles the size of hams. The other was taller, rail thin, and mean-looking.

"What rumors are you talking about?" Virginia pushed through the watching family and ranch hands to stand side-by-side with her brother.

"Mr. Bonneville doesn't appreciate being called a thief," the rail thin man snapped in a whiney voice.

"No one asked you, Brandon," Virginia growled.

The thin man, Brandon, swayed toward her, hands balled into fists. Bonneville reached out an arm to block him with an impatient sigh. "Imagine my distress," he said in a commanding, marginally calmer voice, "when I was dining at the Cattleman Hotel and overheard whispers that I was stealing calves right out of their sweet mothers on the range?"

Jarvis stepped forward to join Howard and Virginia. "More than a few of our cows have come back without their newborns."

"So?" Bonneville shrugged. "Sounds more like carelessness on the part of your ranch hands than anything else."

All three of the Montrose brothers and Luke Chance objected, raising fists and voices.

Franklin let go of Corva long enough to reach out and settle them with a gesture. His movement gave her the strength to stand on her own feet again. No one was paying attention to her anymore. If it wasn't for the circumstances, she would have been grateful to Bonneville.

"Cut the bullshit, Bonneville," Howard said. Before Corva could gasp at his cussing, he charged on with, "Anyone with half a brain knows you've been stealing our calves. Those aren't the only rumors out there. I've also heard that only half your cows ended up carrying in the first place after your bull got sick last spring."

Bonneville sniffed. "I purchased two new bulls in May, and they've performed just fine."

"Shame on you, sir," Elizabeth hissed from the parlor. "There are women and children present."

"So?" Bonneville shrugged. In the process of peering into the parlor, he spotted Corva. A flash of confusion was followed by a scowl as his gaze moved on to Franklin. "And you." He pointed a long finger at Franklin.

"What about me?" To his credit, Franklin stood straight and kept his voice even.

"Going and marrying that little nobody straight off the train." Bonneville huffed in derision.

Franklin slipped his arm around Corva's waist. "I don't see what business it is of yours."

"What business?" Bonneville threw out a hand, appealing to the two men he'd brought with them. "Why, you broke my sweet Vivian's heart. You should have seen the way she carried on when she came home yesterday."

"Blubbed all night," the short, muscled man grunted.

"Shut up, Harvey," Bonneville growled. He resumed his superior air, glaring daggers at Franklin. "Marriage isn't some lark. Men of our status don't just marry any piece of skirt."

Elizabeth and Lucy began to protest, but Corva was too stunned by the boldness of the comment to react.

Bonneville rushed on regardless. "Marriage amongst our sort should be a matter of business, not pleasure. Go to Bonnie's if it's pleasure you want."

Corva was slow to comprehend the chorus of outraged responses from the men and women alike. Bonnie's? A flush painted her face as she realized what kind of an establishment that must be.

"You, sir, should leave my house right now," Howard bellowed.

"I've never heard such shameful talk in the presence of so many women," Virginia said at the same time.

"I made no promise to your daughter, Bonneville." Franklin's simple statement, quietly delivered, hushed the growing madness. Bonneville narrowed his eyes, but Franklin went on. "Any attachment she perceived was a figment of her imagination. In fact, I never intended to marry anyone."

True as she was sure the statement was, it was like a knife in Corva's heart. She had no claim on Franklin's affections, but it seemed that every time she dared to feel even a small bit secure with the situation she found herself in, something came alone to destroy that security. First Franklin's opinion of her paintings, now this.

"Every man says he has no intention of marrying, but we all do in the end," Bonneville said at last. "I could have legal action brought against you for breach of promise."

Franklin merely shrugged. "We don't live in medieval England anymore. It's all water under the bridge anyhow. I've married Corva, and I'll stay married to her. We have calves missing and evidence that they have been taken. By you."

"Evidence?" Bonneville took a half step back. "What evidence?" He shot warning looks to his two companions.

"One of the calves was found," Jarvis said. "With your brand."

"Then it must be my calf." Bonneville dismissed him. "I expect it to be returned with all haste."

"Then I expect our calves to be returned as well," Howard demanded.

Just like that, tensions were high once more.

"You're a troublemaker, Haskell," Bonneville spat. "I know you're only making these outrageous claims because the Hawks play the Bears this Sunday, and you're trying to sway public opinion against us."

Virginia snorted. "Why the hell would Howard go through all that trouble to sway opinion over some silly baseball game?"

Instead of rushing to back her up, every man in the room looked as though she'd turned traitor.

"The Hawks will make a necklace of Bear claws on Sunday," Cody barked.

"If the Bears even have claws to begin with," Mason seconded.

"Like hell they will," Harvey growled. "The Bears will wipe the floor with the Hawks."

"Not if Wilson keeps playing like a girl," Cody declared.

"I beg your pardon?" Lucy snapped. "I can out-hit and out-run you in my sleep."

"Is that what it's come to?" Bonneville sneered. "The best players on your teams are girls?"

Howard glared at Lucy, then at Bonneville. "Lucy only played when we needed a substitute."

"And I did better than half the regular team," Lucy added, crossing her arms.

"This is all beside the point," Virginia hollered over the argument that threatened to break out on top of everything else. "As half-owner of Paradise Ranch, I can promise you, Rex Bonneville, that if we see so much as a hair off of a newborn calf go missing, I will bring the law down on you before you can sneeze."

Silence followed, and then a long, slow laugh from Bonneville. "I'd like to see you try." Half a dozen people opened their mouths to protest, but Bonneville ignored them all. He turned a tight circle and headed out, motioning to his companions. "Come on, boys. We'll leave these mutts to welcome the latest dog to their pack in peace."

He marched out amidst a swirl of objection and protest, slamming the door behind him.

"Don't listen to him, Corva." Alice Flint was by Corva's side, resting a reassuring hand on her arm a moment later. "He's all bluster and unpleasantness."

It took Corva a moment to realize Bonneville had been referring to her. "I—" That was all she could manage.

She was too baffled by the scene that had just unfolded to come up with further comment. She'd only been around Franklin's family for a few hours, and already things had descended into chaos twice.

"Let me fix you another plate." Elizabeth jumped into action.

"We'll move these chairs," Lucy's husband, Gideon, added.

The room burst into activity again, but Franklin stopped it all with a loud, "No, stop, please."

All eyes turned to him in wonder.

"I think I'll just take Corva home," he said. "This has all been overwhelming. A little peace and quiet is necessary."

Corva had never been so grateful to anyone in her life. She even managed a weak smile for her husband amid the volley of protests and promises from his family and friends. Franklin waved them all off, escorting Corva to the door.

"We'll come back tomorrow, when there are fewer people around, so you two can get to know each other," he told his mother as Travis opened the door for them.

"Yes, please." Elizabeth came forward to squeeze Corva's hand. "I'm so sorry about this. That Rex Bonneville makes me so…" She clenched her jaw and shook her head, unable to go on.

"Do you need help with your wagon?" Cody rushed to offer.

Franklin looked like he would refuse the offer, but relented with a sigh. "I might."

He swept Corva out of the house, Cody striding ahead of them to where Franklin had parked. It had grown dark in the time they had been inside, but down the drive, against the last rays of sunset, Corva spotted three men on horses riding away. She doubted that would be the last of the trouble.

Franklin's whole body was aching by the time they returned to the house. The last twenty-four hours were not even close to how he imagined things should be for his new wife. He'd dragged her away from the life she knew back East, dropped her alone in an unfamiliar house for the day, then subjected her to a circus as his parents' house.

"It's not usually like that," he assured her after he settled the wagon and put his horse to bed for the night.

"Not usually so many people or not usually interruptions by irate neighbors?" Corva asked, taking his arm as they started up the ramp to the house.

Franklin huffed a miserable laugh. "I suppose my family is usually out of hand like that. Bonneville was a surprise, though. And I'm sorry about the fire."

They reached the door and he opened it, gesturing for Corva to go through first. She lowered her head and rushed inside, straight to the lamp on the table near the door to light it. Her hands shook as she struck a match to flame and lit the wick.

"I'm usually fine with fire," she said, words and actions an attempt to prove her point. "But not when it's unexpected."

"Perfectly understandable." Franklin crossed to the other side of the room to light the lamps there. He couldn't imagine they'd stay lit long. All he wanted to do was take off his braces and clothes and crawl into bed.

It would be nice to crawl into bed with Corva.

The thought struck him out of nowhere. It was ridiculous, in a way. He was far too tired to engage in any really interesting bedroom activities. No, it was more the thought of having her there, safe in his arms, a comfort to him as well, that appealed to him.

He shook his head and fit the glass back over the lantern. He'd known Corva for one day. She'd come because he let others convince him she needed him. To want to hold her and be intimate with her now was hypocrisy…wasn't it?

"Mr. Bonneville is one of the most intimidating men I've ever met." Corva finished with the lantern but remained facing the table, her hands braced against the edge.

"He's a bully and a menace," Franklin agreed. He sent a longing glance to his bedroom door, then shuffled to the sofa, lowering himself to sit with a wince. "He'll cause trouble, but it's nothing you have to worry about. My family has been dealing with him since he moved out here eight years ago."

Slowly, Corva turned to face him, but kept to the other side of the room. Her lips worked as if she had something to say but was having trouble getting it out. Franklin sat still, encouraging her with a gentle look—not that he had any idea what a gentle look would be.

At last, Corva murmured, "He reminds me of my uncle."

Silence followed. Prickles raced down Franklin's back. Coming from anyone else, those words would be a simple comparison. From Corva, he could see they meant more.

"Was your uncle a menacing bully?" he asked, part of him dreading the answer.

Instead of answering, Corva crossed the room. She sat as tense as a spring on the far end of the sofa. "My uncle was mean, foul-tempered." She stared at her hands, clasped with white knuckles in her lap.

Did she need to confess something? Was she answering his earlier question about her uncle's cruelty? Franklin's heart thumped faster. Could she actually want to confide in him about something, about her past? The prospect thrilled him. She was giving him a chance to be the man he should be.

He shifted to face her in spite of the twinge of pain caused by bumping his braces against the sofa. "He was the reason you were in Hurst Home, wasn't he?" If he could help her to say what she needed to say, then maybe this crazy day would be worth it after all.

Corva nodded. Her eyes glistened with unshed tears. She swallowed hard and dragged her eyes up to meet his. "He was well-respected in his social circles. I was forever hearing what a fine man he was, how lucky my aunt was to marry him. But none of those people knew how he treated us at home."

He didn't want to ask, but he had to. "How did he treat you?" He wanted to reach across the sofa and take her hands, but she was too far away.

"He was free with the back of his hand and his belt with me," she confessed, lowering her eyes. "If I did anything he saw as bad—not fixing his food correctly, being sloppy with my appearance, speaking when I was supposed to stay quiet—he would hit me. Frequently."

"I'm sorry." He did reach for her hand now, but either she didn't see the gesture or was too traumatized by her memories to take the comfort he was offering. He pulled back.

"I learned to bear it as best I could. Painting helped. It was a way I could escape. Things were much worse for my aunt." She swallowed, red splotches coming to her cheeks.

"He beat me, but he did…other things to her. He wanted children of his own, you see, and for whatever reason, my aunt never conceived. But that didn't stop him from trying."

Franklin held out his hand. He didn't need any further explanation, and it was clear that saying even the small bit she had said was too much for Corva. But there was more to say.

"In the last few years, as I grew older, he began to look at me that way too," she continued in a whisper. "He never actually did anything," she rushed to assure him, meeting his eyes for a fraction of an instant. Just as quickly, her gaze dropped. "Other than a few touches here and there."

Fury welled up through Franklin's heart. He wanted to charge off to Nashville to beat the man within an inch of his life, and he wanted to fold Corva in his arms and never let go. But for some reason, being caught between the two, he was frozen and could only listen.

"It was when he started talking more seriously about using me to have his children and somehow passing them off as Aunt Mildred's that things became desperate," she explained. She opened her mouth, stopped, shook her head, then went on with, "That's when a friend told us about Hurst Home. Arrangements were made for me to be secretly moved there, which happened about a year ago."

"And what of your aunt?" His question came out rough and strangled.

Corva lowered her head, face pinched in misery. "She refused to go. Two months after I disappeared, she was found dead, floating in the Cumberland River."

"I'm so sorry."

Corva wiped tears from her eyes. "I can't decide if I'm sorry or not. Maybe it's wicked of me, but if she took her own life or if she met with an accident, then I'm happy for her. She escaped. But if he was somehow responsible…"

"Then the authorities should be involved," Franklin finished when she didn't go on.

"They were involved." She met his eyes again. "No evidence of wrongdoing was found. It was ruled an accident. My uncle was remarried four months later."

Franklin had to clench his teeth to stop himself from calling the blackguard every name in the book. All he managed to say aloud was, "I'm sorry."

Corva took a deep breath, unclasping her hands and smoothing them along her skirt. "My reaction to the fire was bad enough, but when Mr. Bonneville arrived tonight?" She drew in a steadying breath and forced a smile. "Thank you for deciding to leave early. I'm not sure I could have handled staying after that."

"Of course." He stood, painful though it was, because that was the only way he could think to move closer to her. She rose when he did. Her movement was so quick that he couldn't help but wonder if it was a conditioned response to rules her dastardly uncle might have set.

He should step closer to her, put his arms around her, let her rest her head against his shoulder. He should rub her back and speak soothing words to her…the way he had longed for people to speak to him when he lay, broken and suffering, for so many months after his accident. Maybe, just possibly, they could comfort each other.

But no, his damage was his own fault. Hers was cruel injustice inflicted on her by a criminal. There was no comparison. She deserved comfort, he deserved everything he got.

"Everything will be better in the morning," he said

instead of doing what he wanted to do and embracing her. "I'm sure Bonneville will stay away, and you'll enjoy my mother's company one-on-one. She's the steadiest person on this ranch."

For one brief moment, a twist of sadness colored Corva's expression. She swayed on her spot, almost as if she wanted to reach for him. Then she looked away. "Yes, I'm sure you're right."

He had to do something. Every instinct Franklin had screamed at him to be the husband this traumatized woman needed. But how did he do that? How did he even start? He was next door to a stranger to her, and after what she'd just said about her uncle's nefarious intentions, would touching her help or hurt? He'd never known confusion like this before.

"Well," he said at length, his tone far too clipped. "I guess we should turn in for the night so that our better tomorrow can come faster."

She glanced up at him with...with disappointment? No, that couldn't be.

A blink later, her expression softened. "Yes. That would be best."

Neither of them moved. It was his last chance. He needed to move toward her, to open her arms and enfold her, telling her that everything would be all right, that she was safe now, that he would never, ever hurt her, and he would never let anyone else hurt her either.

"All...all right, then," he stuttered. "Goodnight."

His legs were unsteady for more reasons than bones that had been broken long ago as he moved to pick up the lamp, then turn and limp off to his room. A part of his soul hollered at him that he was messing things up again, that he should go back and comfort the woman who had put her trust in him.

But no, he had never gotten things right when he tried to take action where women were concerned. And at the end of the day, Corva deserved someone better than him.

She never should have said anything about her past. Those nightmare days in her Uncle Stanley's house were over. Hundreds of miles separated the two of them, and even if she had stayed in Nashville, her uncle had remarried. He was starting over, and so should she. Talking about the past had only slammed a wall between her and Franklin.

At least, that's what Corva assumed had happened. From the moment she began telling her story, she could sense the tension that swirled between her and Franklin. It had to be revulsion on his part. That was the only explanation. Why else would he keep her at arm's length? He behaved with perfect politeness in the morning and evening when they were together, but shouldn't newlyweds be more intimate? Not that she was in a rush to push herself on Franklin before he was ready. She did like him, though. More and more with each day.

The problem was that he didn't like her.

No, no that couldn't be right. He was polite and kind. But he didn't smile at her as the first handful of days in their marriage slipped by. Then again, she hadn't seen him smile once since she'd climbed down from the train. He had come to her rescue at the disastrous family dinner, but was that just being kind? He would have done the same for anyone. And he didn't like her artwork. She'd caught him staring at one painting or another several times in the first week of their marriage, expression blank. That hadn't stopped her from painting, though, because unlike Uncle Stanley, he hadn't smashed her easel.

"Is everything all right?"

Franklin bumped her out of her increasingly distressed thoughts. They sat side-by-side on the bench of his wagon, driving to church for Sunday services.

"Everything's just fine," she answered. She could feel the heat of embarrassment at being caught wool-gathering.

"You seem a little distant is all." Franklin wore a frown, but it could be concern instead of disapproval.

Corva chewed her lip and tried not to stare at him after he turned his eyes back to the road. She could be reading the situation entirely wrong. Life had given her very little experience of kindness. A part of her clung to the hope that everything she'd been reading into Franklin's actions and conversation in the last week could have been nothing more than the effect of years of her uncle's foulness muddying the waters.

"I'm not sure what to expect from church," she answered after too long a pause. "I haven't exactly made a stellar impression so far."

Franklin shook his head, the corners of his mouth twitching. "That wasn't you. You've done fine. Mother likes you very much."

Corva's face flushed hotter. She'd had a nice tea with Elizabeth Haskell the day after the supper debacle, and

Elizabeth had visited her at Franklin's house to admire her paintings.

"It's not your fault that you arrived in town right as we are having trouble with Bonneville," Franklin went on, his shoulders tightening.

"Will he be at church?" Corva wasn't sure if she was ready to face the hulking man again.

"Probably." Franklin nodded, then reached out to squeeze her knee. "We'll sit with my family and all of our friends. You'll be surrounded by supporters."

"Oh?"

"Yep." He nodded. "I'm sure you'll want to meet Charlie Garrett and his wife, Olivia, and their kids for starters."

Corva brightened. "I would love to meet him. I owe Mr. Garrett so much for maintaining Hurst Home."

"Then there's Dr. and Mrs. Meyers," Franklin went on. "Mrs. Meyers, Emma, is Alice Flint's sister. And they're all very close to Aiden and Katie Murphy. Aiden is the Indian Agent in this area. He and Katie were once captured by Cheyenne."

"Really?" Corva caught her breath.

"It ended well, though. Aiden and Dean—Dr. Meyers—made it their mission to learn to speak Cheyenne, and now they're crucial to the government's dealings with the tribe. Though it to hear Aiden talk about it, it's one of the most frustrating jobs ever. Aiden has the Cheyenne's best interest at heart. The government doesn't."

"I would like to hear his stories someday," Corva answered, and indeed, she would.

As they pulled up to the church, she was already feeling better. It had been restful to stay at Paradise Ranch, alone in Franklin's house for a week, but making friends in her new life would be important too.

It wasn't until Franklin parked in the field beside the church and climbed halfway down from the wagon, struggling as he did, that it dawned on Corva something must have been out of the ordinary. Franklin had a ramp to help him at his house, and one of the ranch hands had been there to assist him at his parents' house, but at the church, it was a different story. She watched from the bench as more than a few churchgoers froze mid-step and stared at Franklin in surprise.

"Franklin Haskell, what are you doing here?" a man with a thick Irish brogue and a red-headed girl of about six in his arms called across the churchyard.

A red-headed woman with him—a baby in her arm and a boy of about four holding her hand—turned to look too. "Franklin?" A beat later, her face lit. "Oh, this must be the wife we've been hearing so much about."

Corva's eyebrows were still raised in surprised as Franklin limped around the front of his wagon in time to nod and say, "Aiden, Katie." He turned to offer a hand to Corva. "They're who I was just talking about."

"I see." Corva took Franklin's offered hand, but did her best to climb down without putting any weight on him. The Murphys were already approaching, so she nodded and said, "Hello," as soon as she was on the ground.

"It's a pleasure to meet you," Katie said, reaching to shake her hand as best she could with a baby in her arms. "Talk in town has been about nothing but you all week."

"Well, you and Bonneville," Aiden added in a quiet growl. As he shook Corva's hand, Corva blinked at the Indian medicine bag he wore around his neck.

Before she could ask about it, Katie waved him off

with, "Ach, don't let's talk about him," and gestured for Franklin and Corva to walk with them toward the church door. "I can't stand the sight of that man," Katie went on. "You've no idea how much trouble he causes around here."

"He stirs things up with the Cheyenne too," Aiden added. He raised a hand to greet another young family, waiting by the church door. "Dean, Emma. Come meet Franklin's new wife."

Corva was whisked into a round of introductions before she even made it inside of the church. Dr. and Mrs. Meyers and their children were sweet, happy people. They, in turn, introduced her to Mr. Kline, the shop-keeper, and Mrs. Patton, who worked as the cook at the Cattleman Hotel. A pretty, young maid from the hotel with Swedish coloring introduced herself as Olga, and after that, Corva began to lose track of the flood of new people.

When she was inside of the church searching for a place to sit, she realized Franklin had fallen behind. A stab of shame over leaving him struck her, but he didn't seem to be in much of a hurry to join the humming, chattering group of friends inside the church. In fact, he only made an effort to climb the church stairs—aided by Travis Montrose, who arrived with his brothers—once Rev. Pickering called people to take their seats for worship.

"Is everything all right?" she whispered to him once they had taken their seats beside Lucy and Gideon's family, the gorgeous, colored light of the stained-glass windows bathing them.

Franklin's lips twitched, and he leaned closer to her to say, "Isn't that what I'm supposed to be asking you?"

A funny tickle formed in her chest, almost as if he'd told a joke. She was more baffled than amused, though.

She sat through the entire sermon, barely able to pay attention. Colored light and dark worry swirled around her. When the sermon was over and everyone rose to head back outside for Haskell's weekly post-church, pre-baseball game potluck lunch, she was determined to ask her question again to be sure Franklin was happy.

"This must be Miss Corva Collier." A tall, handsome gentlemen with dark, greying hair and eyes that danced with mischief approached her before she could form the question. "No, I'm sorry, that would be Mrs. Corva Haskell now."

"Charlie." Franklin nodded to the man, stepping aside so that a few other churchgoers could slip past them. "Corva, this is Mr. Garrett."

That was all he needed to say. Corva turned to the man—his beautiful, petite, blond wife by his side and four adorable children around them—with a beaming smile. "Mr. Garrett, thank you so much for all of your efforts on behalf of Hurst Home. You have…you have no idea how important it is to those of us who live there."

Charlie laughed, banishing whatever tears Corva was tempted to shed. "Believe me, I have an idea. My own background and upbringing were more perilous than I ever want to think about again." He punctuated his remark by laying a hand on his older son's head with a kind of relief in his eyes that only a parent who knew his children were safe could have. "Come outside, Mrs. Haskell, and see what kind of madness we all get up to on Sundays."

Corva was so honored to have this man—a man who had changed her life with his generosity—eager to show her around that once again, she left Franklin behind before she thought better of it.

"The Sunday potluck started back when there were

just a few families here," Charlie explained. "We took turns getting together at each other's houses, but before too long, there were simply too many of us to fit. That's when we started having them at the church. Shortly after that is when the baseball league started."

"We like to enjoy ourselves in Haskell," Mrs. Garrett explained.

"I can see that," Corva answered. She glanced over her shoulder, searching for Franklin. He had fallen behind entirely, and as the Garretts escorted her to a long, high tent that had been pitched—tables of food lined up in the shade under it—she lost track of him. "Franklin?"

Charlie turned to look where she was looking. "He's back there. Honestly, I'm surprised Franklin showed up at all today."

Corva turned to him, brow shooting up. "Doesn't he usually come to church?"

Olivia laughed. "Not nearly enough, and he never stays for the potluck when he does."

"Then why is he here today?" she asked.

Of course, the answer was obvious. Because of her. That didn't answer the question of why he didn't come in the first place. Judging from the crush of people fixing plates of food under the canopy of the tent, everyone in Haskell came out for Sunday events.

Her curiosity stopped cold at the sound of a familiar, female voice. "*My* spinach pie is by far the best thing on this table. I only use the finest ingredients in my cooking."

"Give me a piece, Vivian," another of the Bonneville sisters said. "I simply love your cooking."

Both ladies spoke in overloud voices, as if trying to draw the attention of everyone there. They were both dressed in fine silks, cut in the latest fashions. Two other girls who were just as pretty and dressed just as splendidly flanked them, although one didn't seem to be all that pleased to be part of the spectacle. The Bonneville sisters. Corva would have turned and fled, if Vivian hadn't already noticed her.

"Well, well, if it isn't Mrs. Franklin Haskell," Vivian simpered, even louder than before. "Although, oh my. Where is your husband, Mrs. Haskell? Has he lost interest in you already?"

"I wouldn't be surprised with a skinny, plain thing like her," the sister who had played off of her over the spinach pie said.

"Melinda Bonneville, you know better than that," Olivia scolded her.

"Oh, I'm so sorry, Mrs. Garrett." If Melinda had poured any more sugar into her words, Corva's teeth would have hurt. "I would never dream of saying anything to offend someone as lovely and important as you."

"Maybe not," Charlie muttered so that only Corva could hear, "but I wish those cats would leave my wife alone."

"Poor Mrs. Haskell is so fortunate to make the acquaintance of a woman as refined as you," Vivian agreed. "Perhaps you can give her advice about improving her wardrobe."

Olivia sighed loudly, took Corva's arm, and steered her away from the table with the sisters.

"What?" Vivian called after them. "I meant it as a compliment."

"Not likely," Olivia muttered. "I'm sorry about them. They have more money than they do sense."

"Or manners," Charlie added.

"I met them right after Franklin and I were married," Corva confessed. Charlie and Olivia exchanged worried looks. "Vivian seemed to think Franklin was destined to marry her."

"Well, at least we don't have to worry about *that* silly rumor getting back to you," Charlie laughed. "It's a relief, actually."

"Franklin had no more interest in marrying that woman than he had in marrying—"

Me? Corva thought.

"—a toad," Olivia finished without pause.

"That's what Franklin said." Corva forced herself to smile so that Mr. and Mrs. Garrett would think she believed it. She twisted to search for Franklin in the chattering crowd. "Where did he go?"

"Over there." Charlie pointed to the far end of the churchyard. Every way Corva turned, families were spreading blankets on the grass and sitting down to enjoy their picnic. Franklin had found a seat on a bench facing the yard. Alone. "Why don't you go join him," Charlie said. "Olivia and I will bring you lunch."

"You've done so much for me already, Mr. Garrett," Corva protested. "I can fix plates and take one to him."

"At least let me help," Olivia said.

Ten minutes later, Corva carried two plates, heaping with every kind of delicious food she could imagine, across the yard to Franklin.

"Thanks." He took one plate from her, mouth twitching as close to a smile as he came. "I'm not used to these gatherings, otherwise I would have gotten something for you."

"I don't mind," Corva said, sitting beside him. But a frown came to her face before she could stop it. Actually, she did mind. "These people all seem very nice. Several of them said complimentary things about you."

Franklin hummed doubtfully and shook his head. "They were probably just being nice for your sake."

His comment was so simple, but it froze her, fork halfway to her mouth. She lowered her bite and stared at him. "No one said anything simply to be nice. These are your *neighbors*, and clearly they like you."

As soon as the words were out of her mouth, she regretted them.

"I'm sorry, that came out wrong. I have no business meddling." If her uncle was around, her outburst would have earned her a sharp smack.

But no, he wasn't part of her life anymore. It was high time she learned to say the things that needed to be said.

"I find everyone to be welcoming and warm and eager to include both of us," she managed, then took a bite of chicken to hide the embarrassment that rode hard on the heels of her bravery.

Franklin ate in silence for a few more bites before saying, "Pity is not the same thing as liking someone."

For whatever reason, such a gloomy comment caused something to snap in Corva. She set her plate down on the bench and twisted to face Franklin. "The only person I see pitying you, Franklin Haskell, is you. There have been plenty of times that I felt sorry for my plight in my uncle's house, but as horrifying as it was, I knew the only way I could get out was to stop feeling sorry for myself and to fight. That's why I fled when I had the chance instead of ending up in a river, like my aunt."

Franklin's eyes grew wide during her outburst. By the end, Corva had shocked even herself. Where had that come from?

No, she knew the answer to that. It came from the pain of seeing a good man—a man who had treated her kindly and changed her life—beating himself up. That kind of beating was worse than anything her uncle dished out.

"I'm sorry," she said in spite of the growing conviction in her heart that what her husband truly needed was a firm hand to guide him. "I just don't like to see you punishing yourself."

"I'm not p—" He stopped and blinked, tilted his head to the side. His eyes lost their focus, as if he was looking deep inside of himself and seeing something new.

He was still deep in thought when Vivian and her sisters came flouncing up to them.

"My, my. Are the two of you having a little newlywed spat?" she said.

"We heard you yell at him from our picnic, right over there," Melinda added, gesturing to a quilt that looked to be made of silk draped over a table laden with crystal and china.

"Melinda," the quietest of the four sisters scolded in a whisper.

"Oh, shut up, Honoria. You heard them as much as we did," Melinda snapped.

"You know it's rude to interrupt people's picnics with domestic squabbles," the youngest sister—who couldn't have been more than sixteen—added, crossing her arms and turning up her nose.

"Bebe is right," Vivian said with a toss of her curls. "It's positively upset my digestion to hear a man like Franklin being treated with such disrespect."

Corva's back stiffened and she clenched her jaw. As much as she wanted to defend herself against the groundless accusations, she was loathe to stoop to the Bonneville sisters' level.

"I'm sorry, Vivian, but anything that is said between my wife and I is none of your business," Franklin spoke up. More than that, he set his plate aside, reached for his cane, and pushed himself to stand, pain pinching his face.

All four of the Bonneville sisters took a step back.

"We're sorry," Honoria muttered, head lowered.

"Hush," Vivian whispered, then squared her shoulders and faced Franklin with her nose turned up. "I'm only sorry that you let yourself be talked into marrying this nobody from nowhere."

"Corva is from Nashville, and before that from Atlanta. She is the daughter of a war hero."

Corva's throat squeezed at Franklin's declaration.

Vivian only looked slightly put off. "Well, if you decide you want to get rid of her and marry a woman who can fulfill the social role that is expected of the wife of one of the area's richest ranchers, Papa has a whole cadre of lawyers standing by who could secure an annulment for you."

An annulment? Corva's stomach churned at the thought. If Franklin set her aside, she had nowhere to go, nothing she could do.

But Franklin wouldn't end their marriage. She drew in a breath and stood firm at his side.

"I wouldn't think—" Franklin started, only to be interrupted by Rex Bonneville himself.

"My darlings, what seems to be the trouble here?" he boomed as he strode up to them. He escorted a beautiful woman with honey blond hair, wearing a vibrant blue dress that was cut just a shade too low for a church picnic. The woman didn't look any happier than Corva felt.

"Nothing, Papa," Vivian, Melinda, and Bebe trilled in unison while Honoria lowered her head further and muttered something no one could hear.

"We just came over to greet Mr. and Mrs. Haskell, only to have Mrs. Haskell snap at us," Melinda added, a fiendish glint in her eyes.

Bonneville narrowed his eyes at Corva. That stare and the accompanying intimidation was so close to her uncle that Corva backed up into the bench, nearly losing her balance and sitting on her lunch plate. Franklin shifted to the side, half blocking her from Bonneville's view.

"The conversation is over," he said, quiet but strong.

Bonneville laughed, long and low, from the depths of his chest. "Oh, the conversation is hardly over." There was more menace in his words than Corva thought it was possible for a human to possess.

"*This* conversation is over," Franklin corrected.

Bonneville narrowed his eyes further before his expression resolved to a wolf-like smile. "Girls, your lunch is getting cold. Whatever problems you have with Mr. and Mrs. Haskell can be solved in a gentlemanlike manner when our two teams meet on the diamond this afternoon."

"That's right." Vivian grinned like a snake. "The Bears are ready to thrash your pitiful Hawks and defend my honor."

She didn't wait for a response before turning and swishing away, Melinda and Bebe flanking her. Honoria met Corva's eyes and mouthed the word "sorry" before scurrying off to catch up to them.

"Only a worthless fool breaks a fine young woman's heart the way you broke Vivian's," Bonneville growled, leaning closer to Franklin. "And everyone in this town knows just what kind of a pathetic, cowardly fool you are."

His eyes flared wide with challenge. Franklin remained motionless, but the spark seemed to have left him. As soon as Bonneville saw that, he grinned, then pivoted to stride off after his daughters, chuckling to himself the whole way.

Chapter Seven

If the ground opened up and swallowed him whole, it would be doing Franklin a favor. His heart had already dropped to somewhere near his shoes at Bonneville's threat, not out of fear, but because Bonneville might have a point. Maybe he should consider granting Corva an annulment so that she would be free to marry a man who was worthy of her.

The shock of that thought snapped him out of the gloom he'd mired himself in. Under no circumstances would he ever consider giving Corva up now. She'd looked him square in the eye and given him the dressing down no one—not even Aunt Ginny—had been willing to give him. Heaven help him, he'd had a physical reaction to her scolding that left him wondering if there was a quiet corner close by where no one would disturb them for an hour or so. He needed Corva.

But he had no idea what he was supposed to do next.

He finished his lunch in silence, each bite tasting like ash in his mouth. Corva picked at her food beside him. Not a single citizen of Haskell came forward to bother them, though just about everyone looked on with concern.

As likely as not, they had overheard the Bonnevilles' outburst. More likely than not, they agreed that Corva would be better off getting that annulment.

For the second time in several minutes, Franklin had to exert effort to yank himself out of unhelpful thoughts. But after years of knowing that people looked down on him for the mistakes of his past, it was next to impossible to assume the best. Old habits died hard.

"Hawks, put your plates down, kiss your sweethearts goodbye, and meet at the diamond in five minutes for practice," Mason Montrose called over the heads of the picnickers.

"Bears, we can beat them to it," a second, strapping man with a wild moustache stood and shouted as well.

"Who's that?" Corva asked.

It was such a relief to hear the sweet sound of her voice again that Franklin didn't hesitate before saying, "Keith Frisk. He's Bonneville's foreman and captain of his baseball team. Mason is our captain."

"Oh." Corva nodded, watching as more than just the two teams of baseball players stood and packed away their feast. "Looks like everyone is moving. Should we go too?"

Franklin winced, longing like a knife in his heart. He'd known this was coming, but he'd tried to ignore it all morning. "I don't usually stay to watch the game…"

"Apparently, you don't usually come to church." Corva arched a brow at him.

Franklin gave up with a sigh. "If you want to watch it, I'll come with you."

She answered with a wide smile, hopping up and taking both of their plates. "I've never seen an actual baseball game before." She twisted, searching. "Where should I take these plates?"

"I'll get them," Emma Meyers, whisked forward to take both plates, proving that people were keeping an eye on them. "You two hurry over to the diamond."

An old pain, older than the ache in his legs, gripped Franklin as he reached for his cane and stood. His braces felt particularly heavy as he lurched forward, taking his place by Corva's side. She slipped her hand into his elbow, and the two of them began the slow walk of a hundred yards or so from the church yard to the benches that surrounded the baseball diamond.

"I've got five dollars on the Hawks to win today," Lex Kline told Herb Waters, the livery owner, as the two of them shot quickly past Franklin and Corva.

"The Hawks?" Herb snorted. "How are they supposed to win against the Bears without extra players on the bench?"

"That's right." Lex cursed. "Tony Capponi got that job in Denver and moved on, didn't he?"

They hurried on, out of earshot.

"How many men are on each side of a baseball game?" Corva asked as more people whisked on past them.

"Nine," Franklin answered, "but we usually keep one or two on the bench as relief pitchers, or, when we're playing the Bears, in case of accidents."

"Accidents?" Her eyebrows lifted to her hairline.

Franklin's lips twitched close to a smirk. "The Bears play dirty." He shot her a sideways look. "Are you surprised?"

For a few more steps, Corva blinked, mouth open. Then she loosened her shoulders. "I suppose I'm not. How do they get away with it?"

He huffed. "Chances are, you're about to see."

They reached the edge of the benches. Already, they

were crowded with townspeople. Haskell didn't have a large population—"yet," as Howard always said—but practically everyone was climbing through the stands, finding what they thought was the best spot to cheer on their team. It would have been nice if everyone supported the Hawks, but Bonneville had his friends too, and plenty of people from town liked to cheer for winners, no matter how they won.

Franklin steered Corva toward the back benches at the far end of the Hawk's side.

"Franklin! Corva! Come sit over here."

The surprise of hearing Mason call his name caused Franklin to stumble. Mason stood out on the field, in front of the team bench. He waved to them, pointing at the bench where the Hawk players were tying their shoes and fixing their caps in final preparation for the game.

Searing tension shot down Franklin's spine. It seemed to make the pain from his braces sharper than ever.

"That's okay," he called back, waving them off.

"Come on." Mason started marching toward them. "The team sits together."

Franklin clenched his jaw so tightly that his teeth hurt.

"Are you on the team?" Corva blinked at him.

With a wince that accentuated the dull ache in his chest, Franklin confessed, "Technically, yes."

"Oh." Corva brightened. "Then you should sit with them."

"The team sits together," Mason echoed as he reached them. "You can sit with him and keep him company. Husbands and wives count as one," he added with a wink.

Corva's cheeks splashed pink, and for a moment Franklin wasn't sure if she had taken offense to the comment or not.

"It's a league rule," he quickly explained. "Remember how I mentioned my sister Lucy playing in a game once? It was because Gideon was injured and they needed a replacement."

"We were playing the East End Eagles that time," Mason went on, eyes dancing with mirth. "They agreed to let her play, but, of course, Bonneville balked at the precedent. So the league voted to change the rules so that husbands and wives counted as the same person, in case we ever needed another last minute 'substitution.'"

"I see." Corva relaxed into a smile. "What an interesting rule."

Mason turned to Franklin. "The team sits together. Your spot is right over there."

So much for the diversion of the Haskell League's crazy rules. He wasn't going to get out of sitting in the "place of honor." There was no point in arguing, so with jerky steps, he escorted Corva along the front of the stands to the far end of the team bench.

Several people on the Hawk's side applauded and cheered as they passed.

"What a lovely vote of confidence," Corva commented.

Franklin swallowed his urge to say it was more of a vote of pity.

They took their seats. Franklin did his best not to look like a complete idiot who couldn't keep his balance as he sat. Corva perched by his side, looking this way and that at players and spectators alike.

"I still have so many people to meet and so many names to learn," she murmured.

Behind them, a group of older children started singing a silly baseball song that Katie Murphy had invented based on an old Irish melody. Charlie and Olivia

Garrett and their children arrived and made far more noise than was necessary as they found seats on the bench behind the Hawks. The entire Strong clan—eight children and widower Athos Strong, his long-suffering sister, Piper, with them—claimed the far end of the benches, raising the cacophony to deafening levels.

"I get to play for the West End Wolves next year," Seventeen-year-old Freddy Chance told his friends as they found seats on the bench directly behind the Hawks' team bench.

"I want to play baseball," Franklin's nine-year-old niece Minnie declared, wedging her way between Freddy and Noah Kline, gazing up at Freddy in adoration.

"Girls can't play baseball," Noah growled at her.

"I can." Minnie crossed her arms with a huff, chin tilting up.

"Get out of here, kid," James Plover snapped from Freddy's other side.

"She's okay," Freddy dismissed him. "Let her be."

Corva met Franklin's eyes with a questioning grin.

Franklin leaned closer to whisper. "My niece, Minnie. She takes after Lucy in every way. And she's been following Freddy Chance around like a puppy for years now."

"I see." Corva giggled.

"Practice is over," Rev. Pickering shouted from home plate, fitting an umpire's mask over his head. "Bears, take the field."

The spectators settled and the practicing teams hustled to their respective benches. Keith Frisk pulled the Bears into a huddle for some sort of pep-talk that involved a lot of shouting and pounding his fist into his other hand. Instead of being intimidated by the obvious declaration of mayhem to come, a lump formed in Franklin's throat. It only grew as the Montrose brothers, Luke Chance, Gideon, and the other Hawk players—his father's ranch hands, the men he supervised every day—gathered around the bench.

"We're in for a tough fight today, men." Mason delivered his speech. "We all know the Bears play dirty. Let's be gentlemen, but warriors. Stay clear of them when you can, and swing for the fences."

"Yes, sir," the Hawks answered.

"Now get in there and show them how the game is played."

Franklin's whole body ached with the effort of staying still on the bench as the rest of the team darted around gathering up equipment from practice, sitting in batting order, and as Cody grabbed a bat and approached the plate to lead off. He didn't realize he was gripping the edge of the bench until Corva leaned closer and asked, "Is something wrong? You look like you're in pain."

Franklin forced himself to let out the breath he was holding and sit back. He shook his head. A moment later, the crack of leather hitting wood sounded, and Cody dashed to first base. Lawson Pratt got up to take his turn at bat.

"You used to play, didn't you?" Corva murmured at his side, so close and so soft and so full of pity that Franklin's stomach turned.

He swallowed to keep the pain from overwhelming him. "A long time ago."

The crack of Lawson hitting the ball echoed through the air. All eyes watched it sail into right field, where one of Bonneville's men easily caught it. The Hawk fans groaned in disappointment as the Bear fans cheered.

"Before your accident," Corva said, as though none of

it were as important as the two of them sitting still on the bench.

He kept his eyes forward, watching as Lawson marched back, shaking his head, and as Mason slapped him on the back with a few encouraging words. Travis strode in to take his turn at bat. His first ball was a strike.

Everyone around them focused on the game, so Franklin peeked at Corva, chest and throat squeezing with regret, and said, "I was good once. Really good."

"I'm sorry." Corva rested a hand on his arm.

Franklin swallowed hard, caught between the pleasure of her touch and the pain of his past. "We only had two teams back then, but we still played whenever we could. The game was brand new. Boys who had gone off to fight in the war brought it back when the army deployed soldiers out here to manage the Indians. I was only fifteen and as bull-headed and arrogant as any kid, but I could run fast and steal bases better than anyone. I wasn't a half bad hitter either."

"You miss it." She squeezed his arm.

All he could do was nod. Anything more and he would have risked turning into a watering pot in front of the men who worked for him. That would humiliate him beyond belief.

The sound of the ball being hit drew him back into the game. Travis sprinted on to first and rounded to second while Cody put all his effort into getting to third. Franklin rolled his shoulders and took a few deep breaths, pushing his misery as far back into his soul as it would go.

The Hawks managed to get one run before Travis was tagged out and Gideon fouled out. The Bears came up to bat, and true to form, they tried every nasty trick in the book. By the time the fifth inning was over, the score stood at 3 to 2 in favor of the Hawks, but Lawson was limping after one of the Bears stomped on his foot as he was rounding second, and Cody was nursing some bruised ribs after being hit by the pitcher and walked.

"Crush them," Vivian shouted in a horrifically unladylike voice from the other side of the diamond as Ted Harvey lumbered up to the plate for the Bears. "Rip their heads off!"

"We haven't seen any blood yet," Melinda cried.

Beside them, Bebe laughed, while Honoria hid her face in her hands.

"Well, that answers that question," Corva said as Harvey pounded home plate with his bat, settled into his stance, and glared at the Hawks pitcher.

"What question?" Franklin asked.

She turned to him, a mischievous light dancing in her eyes. "Why none of the Bonneville sisters are married yet. They're so bloodthirsty that a man would be taking his life into his hands to marry one of them."

The laugh bubbled up through Franklin's gut like a spring breaking free of ice in the winter. He tried to stop it, tried to show some respect, but before he could clamp down, ripples of mirth spread up through is chest, hitting his throat with a deep chuckle that caused a smile—a real smile—to crack through onto his lips. His heart expanded in time to the knock of the ball against Harvey's bat.

His reaction didn't go unnoticed. Corva froze, watching him with wide eyes. Her cheeks glowed pink, and a spark flared to life in her eyes that caught his breath in his chest.

He needed to kiss her. The wild thought struck him, banishing every other thought from his mind. He needed more than that. He needed to hold her in his arms, feel her under him, alive with passion. She was so close that one small movement would bring her into his arms. He leaned closer, lips itching to meet hers. Her gaze dropped to his mouth. Just a few inches, and—

"Ohh!"

"Oof!"

"Cheating, cheating!"

The crowd behind them went wild. Freddy and his friends, and several other men and women shot to their feet, shaking their fists.

Franklin gasped and straightened, searching this way and that, as if someone had poured ice water over him then disappeared. A second later, he focused on the action playing out on the diamond.

Billy Martin, their second-baseman, was down, writhing on the ground, clutching his shin, knee bent. Harvey stood on third, laughing up a storm, while the Bears players and fans cheered and shouted. Mason and Travis and half the rest of the Hawks sprinted to second base, where Billy had fallen.

"What happened?" Franklin's heart was ready to beat clean out of his chest for a thousand different reasons.

"Harvey kicked him in the shin as he rounded second," Freddy yelled, shaking his fist at the Bears. "Lousy cheaters!"

"Is he going to be all right?" Corva clasped one hand to her heart. The other gripped Franklin's hand. He hadn't noticed her take it, but he wasn't about to let go.

They strained forward, waiting to see what would happen. Mason and Cody lifted Billy to his feet, but they had to carry him to the bench. Closer to home plate, several Hawks fans and Howard Haskell himself were arguing with Rev. Pickering, but judging by the helpless gesture the reverend kept making, he hadn't seen a thing.

"Excuse me, excuse me, out of the way." Dr. Meyers brushed people aside as he hurried down through the benches to meet Billy, who was laid on the grass behind the Hawk's team bench.

"Keep playing," Vivian screamed from the other side of the field. "Are you men or mice?"

"Play ball," Melinda echoed, just as shrill.

Mason stood as soon as Dr. Meyers bent to examine Billy, and twisted back to the field. "Mike, come in and play second base. Travis, you and Gideon will have to cover the outfield." He turned back to gesture to Cody. "Come on. There's nothing we can do for Billy but win the game."

As big of a thrill as almost kissing Corva had been—although with the light of reason dawning, it would have been scandalous to kiss her in front of most of the town—Franklin's attention was now firmly on the game.

"Is he going to be okay?" he asked Dr. Meyers.

Dean Meyers shook his head. "Ted Harvey is all muscle. I don't think it's broken, but it is bruised. And there's a good chance Billy pulled a tendon when he fell."

Billy let out a string of expletives that had Corva slapping a hand to her mouth. "What about the game?" she asked a moment later.

Dean shook his head. "Billy won't be going back in."

The agony of knowing the game hung in the balance and the Hawks were suddenly short one man was enough to make Franklin want to march over to third base and punch Ted Harvey in the face. At least Mason was able to rally the team to catch the next Bear batsman out for three outs, but at the end of six innings, the score now stood at Hawks 3, Bears 4.

The seventh inning flew by with no runs scored on either side. It wasn't until the eighth that Billy's injury became a serious problem.

"I've got Mike on second and Gideon on first with

one out." Mason worked through the problem, pacing in front of the bench. "Billy is up, but—"

"He's not able to play," Dr. Meyers finished for him.

"And we're short one player." Mason nodded. "Knowing the Bears, they won't let us bat out of order, not even for this."

"You're not short a player." Corva sat straighter. All eyes turned to her. "You've got Franklin."

They all stopped what they were doing. Mason stopped pacing, Lawson stopped rubbing his shin, and the rest of the team on the bench turned to Corva and Franklin with varying degrees of shock and discomfort.

"I'm not an option," Franklin whispered, cursing his crushed legs and the braggart's pride that had destroyed them all those years ago.

"But you're on the team," Corva argued. "You're sitting with the team too. You're a player."

"I can't play," he snapped, each word torture.

"You can't *run*," Corva corrected him.

"Come on," Frisk shouted from behind home plate, where he was playing the position of catcher. "We haven't got all day. Field a player or forfeit."

"You'd love that," Mason growled so that only those nearby could hear.

Corva stood and turned to face Franklin. "You can hit. I can run."

Shock reverberated through Franklin. He reached for his cane and pushed himself to stand, if only so he wasn't the only one sitting at such a crucial moment.

"Don't your rules say that a man's wife counts as the same as him?" Corva argued on.

"That's in case of substitutions," Billy grunted from the grass, where he still sat.

Corva whipped from him to Mason. "Is that what the rules say? Substitutions? Or do they say that they just count as the same player? Because Franklin could bat and I could run."

Mason gaped at her, then scratched his head, then stared into space for a few seconds. He snapped himself out of whatever thoughts he'd had and launched into motion. "It's the only option we've got right now."

He marched over to where several bats were leaning against the end of the bench, selected one, then strode back and handed it to Corva.

Franklin met Corva's eyes, so stunned by the turn of events that his head spun. Lucky for them all, he was also too stunned to protest. He tossed his cane aside and took the bat from Corva. Using it as a cane—along with the support of Corva's arm as she looped it through his—they lurched forward toward home plate.

"We've got a substitution," Mason called out, marching ahead of them so that he reached the plate, Frisk, and Rev. Pickering before Franklin and Corva could. "Mr. and Mrs. Franklin Haskell will be playing in place of Billy."

As soon as the crowd caught on to what was happening, the fans on the Hawk's side burst into wild applause and near insane levels of cheering, while the Bears fans—Vivian, Melinda, and Bebe leading—roared in protest. Franklin could barely hear the exchange going on at the plate until they reached it.

"—within the rules," Rev. Pickering finished whatever he'd been saying with a shrug. "They have every right to play."

Frisk cursed and spit and towered above Franklin and Corva as they found their way into position around home plate, but in the end, as Mason backed off and Rev.

Pickering resumed his spot, he growled, "You won't last an inning anyhow."

The crowd continued to buzz and bristle as Franklin worked out the best way to set himself into batting position on broken legs and braces. His balance was completely off, and it'd been years since he swung a bat at more than just shadows. The first ball came whizzing past, and after the thump of leather hitting leather in Frisk's catcher's mitt, Rev. Pickering shouted, "Strike!"

A nauseous wave of impending humiliation washed over Franklin. He closed his eyes, adjusted his grip on the bat, and swallowed hard. Everyone in town was watching him, looking at him, his braces, his foolishness. Every one of them was likely muttering behind their hands about how much of an idiot he had been to get himself crippled all those years ago, and how he was a fool to think he could compete with the other men now.

The ball whistled past him a second time before he could even take a swing. Frisk swayed to the side, and Rev. Pickering called, "Ball one!"

Cold sweat broke out down Franklin's back. That was a lucky pitch, too lucky. He had to focus, play the game.

His eyes met Corva's for a fraction of a second. She stood with her fists clutched in her skirts—raised to expose her ankles—ready to run. She may have been a woman—a woman who had been through hardship that most people couldn't begin to imagine—but she was ready, poised, strong. She would run to California and back if he hit the ball hard enough.

He narrowed his eyes at the pitcher, his heart swelling in his chest at the thought of Corva running. Every muscle and sinew in his body pulled tight. The Bears pitcher wound up, then threw the ball. Franklin swung for all he was worth.

Crack! The intense satisfaction of the ball hitting the bat poured through Franklin's arms, shoulders, and back with a relief that was close to orgasmic. The ball flew hard, just over the head and outstretched arms of the Bears shortstop. It sailed on, smacking against the ground in left field and zipping through the grass.

"Run," he shouted, though Corva had already taken off.

The crowd exploded in a frenzy of encouragement as Corva bolted for first base. She was absolutely right—she *could* run. He'd never seen a woman run so fast. Her skirts rippled in her wake, and strands of hair flew out of their careful style. Franklin's heart stood still as the Bears left fielder scooped up the ball and threw it. Corva's eyes were glued to the base as she dashed the last few yards. She might have been fast, but she wasn't fast enough. Five yards, four yards, three yards...the ball was sailing faster. The Bears first-baseman reached out to catch it...

...and missed.

The crowd went wild as the throw overshot the base, spinning into the Hawk's team area.

"Run, run," Franklin shouted in elation, waving his arms at Corva to hurry on.

He was taken by surprise as Mike zoomed past him, earning the run that evened up the score. Gideon easily made it to third, but paused to watch—along with everyone else—as Corva sped toward second. The Bears first baseman had recovered the ball and hurled it toward second, but Corva landed—safe and sound—well before the second baseman caught it.

The crowd erupted with joy. Even the Bears fans were on their feet in awe. Franklin would have jumped up and down if he could have. He'd never felt so happy or so proud in his life. He didn't realize he was laughing and shouting until Mason came up and thumped him on the back in congratulations...and to prompt him to move out of the way so Cody could take his turn at bat.

He was completely incapable of sitting down after his and Corva's miraculous turn at bat, though. As Cody stepped up to the plate, Franklin stood just to the side of the bench where Billy and Dr. Meyers sat, Billy's injury forgotten. Cody was good, one of the best players on the team. The Bears were riled up, though. Cody took his position at home plate, took a practice swing, and the pitcher threw the ball with a furious grunt.

It was a bad move on the part of the pitcher. Cody smacked the ball far out into left field. It sailed close to the boundary as Cody dropped his bat and sprinted, Gideon launched toward home, and Corva picked up her skirts and made a dash for third.

The Hawk's fans went wild with cheers as Gideon crossed home plate, moving the score to 5-4 in their favor, but they didn't stop there. Not to be outdone, Corva rounded third and kept on running, her face a mask of concentration. The Bears left fielder caught up with the ball and hurled it toward home.

Franklin's heart stopped and time seemed to slow down as Corva raced the ball, barreling toward home plate. It seemed impossible. Frisk pivoted into position, glove open to catch the ball. He wasn't going to miss the way the first-baseman had, but still Corva ran on. The energy from the crowd was enough to ignite the diamond, Corva's face was red with effort and concentration, but the ball zipped on. Finally, as if sensing it was all or nothing, Corva extended her arms and leapt toward home plate, skirts flying behind her. She skidded across the dirt as Frisk caught the ball and thrust it down.

It seemed to take a lifetime until Rev. Pickering called, "Safe!"

Pandemonium ensued. The game wasn't over, but the Hawks all exploded into cheers and shouts, leaving their positions to run toward Corva at home plate. Mason shot past Franklin, and in spite of all limitations, Franklin limped and staggered along with the team. He moved too fast and lost his balance, stumbling forward, but strong arms caught him and set him on his feet, pushing him on.

Mason and Gideon were lifting Corva to her feet as Franklin reached home plate. She was covered in dust from head to toe, spitting dirt even as she laughed to the point of tears. Ignoring everyone else, Franklin swept her into his arms, planting a solid kiss on her lips. She felt so right, so perfect in his arms. His body flared to life with need that rushed from his groin to his heart, in spite of the crowd around them. No one mattered but Corva, his wife. He didn't even mind the taste of dirt or the mess it made of his clothes as she flung her arms around him in return, kissing him back and sending his senses reeling. They'd done it. They were a team. They'd made each other brilliant.

Chapter Eight

Corva had never been happier in her life. That was all there was to it. Her muscles ached from the bruises she'd sustained sliding into home as Franklin drove back to the ranch, she was covered with dirt and dust from head to toe, and her best dress was torn in several places, but her heart was so light it threatened to float right out of her and carry her to heaven. And to top it all off, Franklin had kissed her with a passion that had made her dizzy and tingly.

"I can't believe we won," she giggled. "We actually won."

"I'm just sorry that you couldn't have scored the winning run," Franklin said. "That ninth inning was a bit of a let-down after the eighth."

"It doesn't matter. We still won." She turned her face up to the setting sun as she spoke, letting joy wash through her.

"We did," Franklin echoed her, smiling.

That was far and away the best part. Franklin was smiling, really and truly smiling. His smile was like the first buds of spring as they popped up through long-dormant ground. It was like the warmth of the hearth as bread baked. No, something about it was hotter, hungrier, and focused on her. Franklin's smile confirmed something else that she had suspected since she first set eyes on him at the train station. Her husband was the handsomest man she had ever known. With his troubles broken and sorrows lifted, that fact was clear as day. It was almost like meeting him anew. Body and soul, she wanted to know this man more.

"Aren't we a fine mess, though?" She continued to giggle as Franklin pulled the wagon to a stop next to the ramp on his property.

"We definitely need a bath." He echoed her mirth.

"I'll go inside and fill the tub." She hopped down before he could come around to escort her. In her heart, she knew they were well beyond that sort of polite gesture. If the day had proven nothing else, it had shown that they were a team and that they functioned best when they worked together, each doing what they could do.

Corva skipped up the ramp to the front porch, through the door, and flittered about the main room, lighting the lamps. The house had only a small water closet—nothing like the single, serviceable washroom that Hurst Home had. It was a step up from an outhouse and outside water pump, but she still had to drag the huge, brass washtub out from the kitchen closet and position it near the fireplace in the living room.

By the time Franklin came in from settling the wagon and horse, she had the tub partially filled with room-temperature water, and the kettle and several pots of water boiling on the kitchen stove. Franklin hung his cane and hat on the peg by the door, and set to work lighting a fire in the fireplace to take the spring chill out of the air.

"I hope it won't bother you to have this so close to the

tub," he called as Corva watched the water boiling on the stove in the other room.

"Fire only bothers me when it's unexpected or out of control," she answered. "The bigger problem is how we can both fit in the tub to wash up at the same time."

Her comment was meant to tease, but the moment the words were out of her mouth, images of the two of them squeezing into the tub together, slippery and without clothes, rushed to her mind. She flushed with embarrassment and slapped a hand over her mouth, hoping Franklin didn't think she was impertinent. But at the same time, the image seemed so enticing, so exciting, so right.

A long silence followed before he called back, "That would be something, wouldn't it?" His voice was low and rough, with a note of something…something *spicy* in it.

A slow shiver began at the bottom of Corva's spine and spread through her in warm waves. She waited until the water on the stove was at a full boil before wrapping a towel around the handle of the biggest pot to carry it into the main room and over to the tub.

Her plan was to avoid Franklin's eyes, in case he could glean the intimate nature of her thoughts. He was her husband, with all that entailed, but shouldn't she wait for him to act on the sizzling energy between them that their kiss on the baseball diamond had sparked? The plan to avoid looking directly at him went out the window when their eyes met. Franklin practically glowed with admiration for her as he set up a tall, painted screen between the tub and the sofa.

They regarded each other in charged silence for a moment before Franklin cleared his throat and said, "I figure we can take turns." He unfolded the screen all the way. "You go first and I'll wait on the sofa, then I'll wash."

Twin feelings of excitement and disappointment flooded Corva from both sides, leaving her stunned and shy. Was she wrong about the energy pulsing between them? She marched up to the tub and emptied the boiling water. Maybe she had imagined the hunger in his eyes on the wagon ride home, was imagining it now. She knew so little about intimacies between men and women that she could be getting it all wrong.

"I suppose everyone in town will know who I am now," she made conversation to hide her uncertainty, returning to the kitchen to get the other pot and kettle of boiling water. She didn't want to be wrong about the shift in their relationship.

Franklin chuckled. "No doubt."

He had already removed his jacket and laid it over the arm of the sofa as she carried the pot and kettle to the tub, and now sat, removing his braces. Corva was sorely tempted to watch him peel them off completely, but if she wanted a bath that was even a little warm, she needed to boil more water.

"I take it that sort of thing doesn't usually happen in baseball games." She carried the pot and kettle back to the kitchen to refill and reheat.

"I should say not," Franklin laughed.

The instinct to read volumes into that comment had Corva clenching her jaw in frustration with herself. Why was it so easy to believe people thought the worst of her and so hard to accept compliments when they came?

"The best part is that the Bears lost," Franklin continued, shuffling something in the other room. "That ought to keep Bonneville quiet for a while."

"It won't make him twice as mad about the calves?" She dipped her fingers in the water to test how fast it was heating, then crossed to the doorway to wait.

Her heart stopped beating and a shiver passed through her at the sight of Franklin standing in front of the sofa, facing to the side, with his shirt and shoes off. He'd removed the braces from his legs too, and stood there in nothing but his trousers. Aside from those trousers being crumpled where the braces had been buckled, he looked every bit a whole, fit man.

"Possibly," he went on, not seeing her watching him. "But it's just as likely he'll lay low for a while to avoid any sort of talk with his name in it."

He turned to face her. Their eyes met. Swirls of warmth of a sort she'd never felt before pulsed through her. It was too complex to call admiration. All Corva knew was that she wanted to keep looking and looking at her husband, and more. The look was in his eyes too, growing fiercer by the moment.

"Sorry." He twisted as if he might reach for something to cover himself, but without his braces, he wobbled dangerously and had to hold still to regain his balance. Once he had, he lifted his arms in a helpless gesture. "I hope you don't mind. We are married, after all."

"I don't mind." Her voice came out in a rough squeak. She couldn't tear her eyes away from him—the lean lines of his torso, the broadness of his shoulders, the dusting of dark hair that converged into a line below his navel and ran down to his waistband. The contours below his waistband.

She was saved by the bubble of boiling water on the stove behind her, and whipped around, rushing to the stove. Her cheeks were far hotter than the kettle and pots, and so were other parts of her. The ache and pull inside of her was both exciting and nerve-wracking. Was she supposed to feel that way at the sight of a man's chest?

The blessedly few times she'd caught her uncle in a state of undress had inspired revulsion, not this...yearning.

"Don't be ridiculous," she whispered to herself, grabbing the larger pot from the stove.

When she returned to the main room to pour the water into the tub, Franklin had moved to a cupboard at the side of the room and was searching through cakes of soap, towels draped over his bare arm. Heaven help her, but his back looked as good as his front, not to mention his backside. She rushed back into the kitchen to fetch the rest of the water before her thoughts drifted any further.

By the time she poured out the last of the boiled water and returned the empty vessels to the kitchen, the main room was far hotter than she remembered.

"I've set the towels and soap on a stool by the tub," Franklin said as he walked carefully to the sofa on the other side of the screen from the tub. "There's a washcloth for you draped over the side of the tub. Don't worry about getting dirt on the floor as you undress. We can clean that up later. Do you need help with buttons?"

A hitch caught in Corva's chest. She had done up the buttons herself, so she could undo them too, but that nervous, excited part of her nodded and stepped forward. Her heart raced a mile a minute as she reached him, then turned her back to him.

His fingers brushed the back of her neck as he undid the top button of her high collar, and a bolt of electricity zipped through her. "How accomplished of a seamstress are you?"

"Hmm?" His feather-light touch as he worked on her buttons was too much of a distraction for her to form a real answer, or comprehend what he'd asked. His warm, throaty chuckle that followed didn't help her focus at all.

"I don't know much about women's dresses, but this

one looks like it's had it." His hands reached the curve of her spine between her shoulder blades. "You can try to repair it if you want, but I'm more than happy to buy you a whole closet full of new clothes. That's actually something I've wanted to talk to you about."

"Oh?" The single word came out as a shaky trill.

He paused as he reached the top of her chemise. For a moment, even the air stood still. He leaned closer to her. Corva could feel his heat, feel the whisper of his breath against her neck. His hands continued down, undoing buttons, slower, as if savoring each one.

"I'm your husband." His voice was heavy with promise, the words tickling against her skin with such intensity that she tensed. "I'll give you anything you want, all you have to do is ask."

Her dress sagged loose around her as he finished with the buttons at her waist. She gasped, rippling with longing, as he slid his hands around her waist to her stomach against the stays of her corset. His lips brushed the side of her neck, sending a flash of fire through her. She'd seen firsthand the power that fire could have, but never had she imagined that she would want to surrender herself to it.

He moved one hand away from her waist, brushing up her side, then pushing her dress off her shoulder and down her arm. His lips followed, tracing a line from her neck to the top of her arm. Each gentle kiss filled her with more and more of a sense of need. She needed him in far more ways than as her protector and provider.

She let him slide her sleeves down her arms one at a time, then with a tenderness that left her trembling, pushed her dress and petticoat over her hips. They spilled like a puddle to the floor. His bare arms circled around her, the heat of his skin raising gooseflesh on hers. He spread a hand over her stomach, easing her back against him, while his other hand rested on her hip with a heady mixture of reassurance and possession.

"Sh-shouldn't we bathe?" Corva winced as soon as the words were out. Her heart didn't want to stop this beautiful, new exploration, it wanted to run headlong into it.

"You're right," Franklin murmured against her ear. "*We* should."

The dark timbre of his voice sent another wave of trembling through her. It was only just settling and spreading through her when he inched back and twisted her to face him. Her split-second of disappointment blossomed to a physical ache at the sight of his eyes, glowing with heat and need and things she couldn't begin to put a name to. He leaned toward her, and for a glorious moment, she thought he would kiss her. At the last second, he stopped himself, lowering his eyes.

He took her hand, steadying her as she stepped out of the pool of her discarded clothes, then led her around to the other side of the screen. The fire in the fireplace crackled merrily, and a faint wisp of steam rose from the fragrant water in the tub.

"We're not both going to fit," she whispered, heart fluttering.

"No, we're not," he agreed. It didn't seem to bother him. He reached for her waist, pressing her corset to unhook the front inch by inch.

Corva's head spun with desire as he freed her, tossing her corset aside. He brushed her waist with both hands, and just when she thought she might turn liquid with expectation, he slipped his hands under the worn cotton of her chemise and lifted it up. She was so startled by the sudden gesture that she raised her arms, letting him pull the garment up over her head. That left her standing in front of him in nothing but her drawers.

"You're so beautiful," he whispered. He leaned toward her, brushing her lips with his as his hands searched for the tie of her drawers.

One tug and a push, and she was standing before him naked. He swayed back to look at her. No one, no man, had ever stood gazing at her naked body. She fought the urge to cover herself, her breath catching in her throat as she realized she would much rather have him cover her instead. She wanted to feel his hands on her body in all of those special places reserved for a husband.

Instead, he bent carefully to the side, taking up a washcloth and dipping it in the warm water. When he straightened, he brought the washcloth to her shoulder and squeezed. Tendrils of water slithered along her overheated skin, running in rivulets around her breast, down her back, reaching the curve of her belly and disappearing into the curls between her legs. She gasped, and Franklin sucked in a breath, the heat in his eyes flaring as he followed the trails of water down her body. He stooped again, unsteady, to wet the cloth, then squeezed water over her other shoulder. It tickled across her skin, causing prickles and aches. Her breasts grew heavy, her nipples tightening. The pressure between her thighs was almost unbearable.

"Franklin," she whispered, unsure if it was a plea or a prayer.

"I could look at you like this all day," he murmured, his eyes devouring her. "You're perfect." He dropped the washcloth, sliding his hands over her wet hips and up her sides to cup her breasts. She watched the path he traced, noting the bulge that had formed in his trousers. It made her knees weak and the ache between her thighs flare. "But I don't know how much longer I can stand."

She caught her breath when he lowered his eyes. His hands remained on her breasts, his thumbs stroking her nipples. "We could…" She swallowed, licked her lips. "We could go to your bed."

His eyes flickered up to meet hers, shining with desire. "We could."

Still, he didn't move. "I…I want to."

That sealed it. He surged into her, mouth meeting hers in a kiss that seared her to her soul. Too many new, wonderful sensations struck her at once—the play of his tongue against hers, the press of her breasts against his bare chest, the pressure of that hard part of him against her hip. She wanted all of it at once, and she wanted to experience each part on its own. He brushed a hand down over the small of her back, caressing her backside and teasing his fingertips along the cleft to the point where she let out a sound of pleasure she hadn't known she could make.

Franklin swayed into motion. It was difficult for him to move fast without his braces, but with Corva helping, they shifted into the bedroom, rolling onto Franklin's bed. He stretched himself over her as she lay on her back at first, kissing her lips, her jaw, and her neck, while his hand teased her breast to the point where she hummed with pleasure. But when he reached for the waist of his pants, his coordination faltered and he dropped to her side, blowing out a frustrated breath.

"Let me," she whispered, fighting to hold onto her confidence.

Franklin relaxed onto his back, and she lifted to her knees beside him. Her heart thundered in her chest. She'd never even dreamed of undressing a man before. Her hands shook as she unclasped the fastening of his trousers. She licked her lips as she pushed them open and pulled at the ties of his undershorts. When everything was loose around his hips, she gathered her courage and drew them down.

Franklin gasped as the stiff, strange part of himself burst free. Corva blinked, a shiver sliding down her back and swirling through her core, as it sprung up, laying against his abdomen. His shaft was flushed and thick and as long as her hand. The tip flared and glistened with moisture. A flash of fear cut through her, but just as quickly it was overpowered by curiosity, the need to touch, and the desire to know what it meant and what it could do. She tugged Franklin's trousers down his legs, so eager that she almost didn't see.

One flickering glance to his thighs and calves as she pulled his trousers all the way off, and Corva froze, her heart breaking. Franklin's legs were a scarred mass of crisscrossing lines. His muscles tensed beneath his damaged skin, creating uneven plains and curves, as if they had healed wrong over bones that no longer ran the way they were supposed to. One of his knees wasn't where it should have been, and the ridges of his shins were broken and scarred. Bruises peppered his flesh where his braces must have pinched.

"Oh, Franklin," she whispered. It was a wonder he could walk at all.

Franklin cleared his throat and propped himself on his elbows. "Please don't look," he said, voice filled with a decade of regret. "Please don't—"

He sucked in a breath as she stroked from his calf to his thigh.

Corva flinched back. "Does that hurt?"

He shook his head, and, if Corva wasn't seeing

things, his staff twitched. "No one has touched my legs since—"

She dared herself to run her fingers from his calf to his thigh again. He let out a low growl and lowered himself to his back, closing his eyes. Corva repeated the touch, exploring further, and eliciting the most exciting sounds from him. Her body warmed and came alive again at the suggestion that she was giving him pleasure.

She ventured higher with her strokes, biting her lip as she caressed the tight sack beneath his shaft, then brushed her shaking fingers up his length. Franklin gasped, his eyes flying open. He jolted into action, capturing her and drawing her up alongside him, then twisting so that she was on her back with him above her before she could catch her breath.

"What?" She panicked. "Did I do something wrong?"

"No." He nestled between her legs, prompting her to spread her hips so that he fit more closely. "It's only that I'm too aroused already, and once a man reaches a certain point, he can spill his seed before he's ready."

Corva opened her mouth to ask a hundred questions in one, but Franklin silenced her with a kiss. She sighed as their lips met, their tongues touched. Their bodies seemed made to slide together. Her skin was still damp, but whether from the bathwater or sweat she was no longer sure. All she knew was that it was bliss itself to press into him, flesh meeting flesh, and to circle her arms around him. No one had ever told her what to expect from her husband in bed, but her body knew at least part of what it wanted. She opened her hips more and more on instinct alone as Franklin ground against her.

His hand reached between them, caressing her thigh and pushing it wider. It felt so wonderful, so right, that she hummed in response, pressing her fingertips into his back. When his fingers delved between her legs, she sighed and arched toward his touch. He brushed across a part of her that flared with pleasure more intense than anything she'd ever felt, and she bucked and cried out.

"Good," he whispered against her neck, and continued to circle around that spot.

Corva closed her eyes and tilted her head back, pressing into his hand as he stroked pure joy through her. Their bodies were so close, so many parts of them touching. He nipped at her neck, his teeth a revelation. But more and more of her focus was on the ache between her hips that pitched higher and tighter and stronger until something within her burst into a flood of pulsing pleasure.

She was still riding high on the waves of that pleasure when he shifted above her and thrust. Her eyes flew wide as an impossible fullness joined the softening waves of pleasure within her. Was there a twinge of pain? She couldn't tell through the rightness of it. Franklin groaned deep in his chest, and she felt that stretching, hot fullness thrust again and again and again. The waves of pleasure that had ridden themselves out pitched again, and she found herself crying out with each of his thrusts.

All at once, he sighed above her, then slowly, gradually, his rocking thrusts drained of power as he came to rest on top of her. For a brief, perfect moment, he rested his full weight on her. It was crushing, but there was something beautiful in it. She was all his, inside of her and around her.

At last, breath shaky, Franklin withdrew and rolled to the side. He reached for her, drawing her close and positioning her against him, in spite of the intense heat that still flared between them. To Corva, it felt perfect. Her body was limp and stretched in the most amazing ways, but it was her heart that felt the deepest change. She may have been a bride before, but now she was a wife.

Franklin awoke bright and early the next morning to a sensation he hadn't felt in years—contentment. Yes, his legs ached a little, he had a full day of ranch work ahead of him, and chances were that Bonneville would cause some sort of trouble. But he was warm and relaxed in bed, and he held his sleeping wife in his arms.

Corva fit so perfectly against him. He smiled and planted a soft kiss on her shoulder at the memory of all they'd shared the night before, careful not to wake her. He'd be lying if he said he hadn't thought about what it would be like to take her to bed, but the reality of the two of them together was a thousand times more precious than anything he had imagined. Most importantly of all, she had seen his legs, seen the scars and the bruises, and wanted him anyhow.

He slipped out of bed as silently as he could, checking constantly to be sure he didn't disturb Corva. He was always a little unsteady in the morning, but as he crept around the bed, grabbed clean clothes, and snuck out into the main room, using the rails built into the wall to stay upright, it was as if his heart gave him wings.

The mess that waited for him by the fireplace brought him firmly back to earth with a thud. His brass bathtub still sat by the fire, the water cooled to room-temperature. The floor was still soggy in spots around it, and Corva's ruined, dirty dress lay in a sodden heap on the floor. Her chemise and drawers were still damp from the way he'd sluiced water over her shoulders, watching it trickle down the full curves of her—

He sucked in a breath to stop his body's reaction at the images flooding his mind. He had work to do, and it would be impossible if he got carried away and slipped back into bed with his wife. His beautiful, perfect wife.

The best way to combat ill-timed desire was to work it off. Franklin moved to the sofa to dress, then strapped on his braces, which still sat on the floor where he'd left them. Normally, he would wait until the last minute to put them on, but one look around the room told him he would need extra strength that morning.

By the time Corva stepped out of the bedroom, dressed in one of her simple work dresses, her hair pulled back in a braid, Franklin had emptied the tub, moved their old clothes to the laundry basket, and was mopping the floor. He paused what he was doing to tell her, "Good morning."

"Good morning." A pink blush tinted her cheeks, and she glanced down, smiling from ear to ear.

Her modest beauty took Franklin's breath away and left him seriously debating forgetting about work and spending the rest of the day in bed with her.

"Are you hungry?" she asked a moment later, shaking herself out of her shyness and crossing the room to the kitchen. "I should have gotten up earlier to start breakfast. Something hearty this morning, I think."

Franklin abandoned his mop to follow her. He caught up to her at the kitchen counter, closing his arms around her. Corva gasped at his touch, then turned to face him. He swept her into an embrace, and slanted his mouth over hers in a kiss that would say far more than any feeble words he tried to put together.

She relaxed into him, resting her head against his shoulder for a moment when he ended their kiss.

"Yes," he murmured, settling his hands at her waist,

loving the feeling of her against him. "Something hearty is definitely in order."

He kissed her again, then let her go, though it took a colossal effort. How did husbands across the world ever let their wives go once they had them in their arms?

The answer came in the form of a room that needed him to finish cleaning it and a breakfast that wouldn't make itself. The work was easy now that he had this new song in his heart. He was certain that everything else in his life would be bright and new too.

"I might try riding out with the boys to manage the herd today," he told Corva as they sat across the breakfast table together. Suddenly, sharing every detail of his daily life with her was vital. "Maybe if Bonneville sees that we're serious about keeping an eye on our cattle, he and his men won't try anything funny. Not that they'd dare try anything after yesterday."

"I suppose not." Corva pushed her eggs around her plate with her fork, her cheeks still as pink as roses.

"It's calving season anyhow, so we're likely to see a few more born on any given day. The sooner we can get them back to the barnyard where they can be tended to, the better."

"Yes." She reached for her coffee, not meeting his eyes.

"I'll try to get back here early tonight for supper," he went on, a long-forgotten smile spreading across his lips. It felt so good to smile. It felt good to share. "Not sure what we could fix to eat, but we'll find something."

"I…I could go in to the mercantile and do some shopping," Corva offered.

"What a grand idea. That way you can get out of the house a bit and maybe even see some of the people you met yesterday." He pushed his chair back and stood, carrying his plate and coffee mug to the kitchen. He glanced across one of Corva's paintings that hadn't been hung as he went. It leaned against the wall as if waiting for a home. "Maybe you could take some of your paintings with you," he suggested. "I bet Lex Kline would be willing to sell them in his store. You might be able to make some decent pocket money while you're at it."

A long pause followed as he deposited his dishes in the sink before a small, hesitant, "Yes, maybe," floated through the doorway.

Franklin frowned. That didn't sound right. Corva was happy this morning. Shy, but happy.

He left the kitchen and crossed to the front door and the peg where he hung his work hat and his cane. Corva was still seated at the table, staring at one of her paintings on the wall across from her seat at the table.

"Everything all right?" he asked, a twist of uncertainty in his gut.

She sucked in a breath and shook herself out of whatever thoughts she had. "Fine." She stood, hurrying to gather her things and clear the table.

Franklin reached for the doorknob, but hesitated. Was it his imagination, or was she not looking at him? Was she upset? Had he somehow hurt her last night in his ardor? He searched back over everything that had happened between them, looking for any sign that she hadn't been as swept away with passion as he had been. Nothing at all indicated that she'd been uncomfortable with their love-making.

He glanced to the clock on the wall by the dining table. "I need to get over to Dad's house," he said, regretting the words. "We'll talk later, when I get home."

Corva was still fussing with the breakfast things

around the table, but she glanced up, smiled briefly, and nodded. "All right. Enjoy your day."

He smiled back, glad that he could at least do that now that she'd broken through the misery around his heart. Then he fit his hat on his head, gripped his cane, and headed out the door. Whether there was trouble or not—and how could there be after such a dazzling night?—Franklin was only sure of one thing. He had a lot to learn about women. He had a lot to learn about his wife.

Chapter Nine

The war that was taking place in Corva's heart was hard to ignore and impossible to brush away by telling herself she was being silly. She and Franklin had shared something special the night before, something amazing. So why had he acted so...so *normal* this morning? They'd shared a kiss in the kitchen, true, but then he'd gone on to talk about ranch business? He'd dashed off to work without a single lingering glance or sweet words. He hadn't told her he loved her.

She shook her head and sucked in a breath as she pushed away from the kitchen sink, dishes washed and dried. Growing up with her aunt and uncle had taught her nothing about how a marriage should work, but surely, if the intimacies she and Franklin had shared meant as much to him as they had to her, he would have behaved differently somehow, wouldn't he? She just didn't know enough to rest perfectly easily.

And he'd told her to get rid of her paintings.

That was like an arrow in her heart. She walked into the main room and looked around at her artwork—her comfort and her friends. He wanted nothing to do with them, wanted them out of his house. Corva clutched a hand to her heart, fighting off the sensation that in order to be safe and loved by her husband, she had to give up part of who she was and blend into his life entirely.

"It's worth it," she whispered, crossing to the small stack of paintings she hadn't hung yet. But even though the words passed her lips easily, her heart squirmed and wrestled with the idea. Safety was a wonderful thing, but was anything worth losing herself?

When she stepped outside, two paintings under her arm to take to the mercantile, she was surprised to find the wagon hitched and ready for her to drive. She stopped and stared at it for a moment. If the wagon was here, waiting for her, how had Franklin gotten to his father's house? Could he have walked all that way, just so she could have the wagon?

The idea seemed preposterous, but there was the wagon, all for her. She wasn't about to let it go to waste. With her paintings under one arm, she marched over and climbed up. Corva didn't consider herself the best driver, but she'd run errands for her aunt and uncle through the crowded streets of Nashville enough times to manage it. Driving across wide open plains was far easier than navigating city streets. Even when she reached the outskirts of Haskell and the livery where people from the outlying ranches parked on visits to town, she was able to coax the horse to a stop.

"Whoa, whoa there. Good morning, Mrs. Haskell." A cheery-faced man stepped out of the large stable and approached Corva to lend a hand.

"Hello?" Corva answered uncertainly.

The man gave Franklin's horse a quick pat, then rushed to help her down. "Herb Waters, ma'am," he introduced himself, and before Corva's feet could touch the ground, went on to say, "That was some mighty fine baseball you played yesterday."

A hot blush flooded Corva's face, and she looked down. "Thank you. It was…unexpected, to say the least."

Mr. Waters laughed and clapped her shoulder a little harder than was proper. "I don't suppose you could see the look on Rex Bonneville's face when you went sliding into home, but it was a sight, I can assure you."

"Oh…I…" Corva bit her lip, no idea what to say.

"Me and the boys had a right laugh about it after the game over at the Silver Dollar. It's just a shame you couldn't join us." He continued to chuckle and snort and shake his head as he stepped back to see to the horse.

"The Silver Dollar?" Corva asked, turning to retrieve her paintings and her reticule.

"That's right, I forgot. You're new in town," he said over his shoulder as he worked to loosen the horse's harness, still chuckling. "The Silver Dollar is the saloon. We don't see many ladies in there. Women, yes. Ladies, no."

Corva flushed deeper. "Oh." No ladies, and yet this man she didn't really know had clapped her on the shoulder, like she was one of the boys, one of the team. Well, in a way, she was. She should take it as a compliment.

"You go along and run your errands, Mrs. Haskell," Mr. Waters said. "I'll take good care of Franklin's rig here."

"Thank you." It was all Corva could think of to say. She gave the overly friendly man a smile, secured her paintings under her arm, and walked through the livery gate and out into the main street of Haskell.

"Good morning, Mrs. Haskell," a young man hard at work pounding what looked like a horseshoe on an anvil called out to her as she passed. "Excellent run you scored yesterday."

"Thanks," Corva called back to him, striding on.

"Morning, Mrs. Haskell," another man who sat outside a saddlery, fashioning something out of leather in the morning sunlight greeted her. "Top-notch game yesterday, don't you think?"

"Yes, it was." Corva smiled and nodded, then picked up her pace.

"Oh! Good morning, Mrs. Haskell." A young woman wearing not much more than a gathered skirt, chemise, and corset waved to her from the porch of a pink building with a sign that read "Bonnie's" over the door. Two other young women in similar states of undress, their hair loose, and rouge on their cheeks jumped up to join the first at the porch rail. "We were all so thrilled to watch you play in the game yesterday."

"Franklin sure scored a winner with you," one of the other girls called.

Corva nearly missed a step. *Franklin?* She might have been inexperienced in the ways of the world, but she knew a whorehouse when she saw one, and the girls were on a first-name basis with her husband?

"Thanks," she called back to them, far more shaky than she wanted to admit, and rushed on.

By the time she made it to Kline's Mercantile, her heart was pounding and a sheen of sweat had broken out down her back. It was one thing to live in a cheerful, exuberant town where everyone knew her name and greeted her as she passed, but it was quite another to be praised for her athletic accomplishments by complete strangers. Of all the things that could have given her a name.

She glanced down to the paintings under her arm. They were who she was, who she always thought she'd be, not some sports hero. When had she stopped being Corva Collier and started being Mrs. Franklin "Baseball" Haskell?

She cleared her throat, took a deep breath, and steadied herself by perusing the aisles and shelves of goods for sale. Kline's Mercantile was a cozy and well-stocked store. It only took Corva a few minutes of studying shelves of canned goods, a table of fabric bolts, and a row of flour, sugar, and grain sacks to settle back into the wife she knew herself to be. There were groceries to buy and responsibilities to see to. That was something familiar. The bell over the front door jingled a few times as she looked, but she paid no mind to the other customers that came in or their quiet conversations.

"Ah, Mrs. Haskell," the man behind the counter greeted her as she finished her second circuit of the store. "What can I help you with today?"

"Franklin and I need a few things," she replied, startled that her voice was so quiet and cowed. That wouldn't do at all. She cleared her throat and went on with, "And...and I was wondering if you might be interested in selling a few paintings of mine here in the store."

She was certain her heart would break at the prospect, but when Mr. Kline brightened and held out a hand for one of the paintings, a zip of excitement took her by surprise.

He took one of the landscapes she'd painted using a picture in a book and her imagination and held it up. A smile spread slowly across his face. "You did this?"

Corva's throat closed up in anticipation, so she could only manage a nod.

"I've never seen such excellent work with my own eyes."

"Really?" Her voice pitched to a near squeak.

Mr. Kline grinned at her. "Let me see the other one."

She handed over the second painting she'd brought — a view out her bedroom window in Nashville depicting a rainy day and the bedraggled maid from the house across the street. It was a sad painting, but Corva considered it among her best work.

Mr. Kline let out a long, low, "Ohh."

"Oh?" she echoed, uncertain.

"That…" He nodded at the painting and the poor, grey maid. "That's beautiful, in a sad sort of way. Looks like you're good at more than just running bases."

He winked at her, then held up both paintings, glancing between them. Corva's heart filled with joyous relief, nearly lifting her off her feet…

…until a bark of, "That's the most pathetic thing I've ever seen," from behind her brought her crashing down.

She turned to find Vivian and Bebe Bonneville standing behind her, arms crossed, sour expressions on their faces.

"Yeah, they're pitiful," Bebe echoed her sister's comment.

Mr. Kline lowered the paintings, fixing the Bonneville sisters with a stern frown. "Miss Vivian, Miss Bebe. What can I do for you?"

"You can start by not patronizing *that* sort of person." Vivian brushed past Corva, knocking her off-balance as she went. "I also need three yards of this lace." She thrust a card of lace at Mr. Kline.

Mr. Kline sighed, sending Corva an apologetic look as he put her paintings down. He reached for a pair of scissors under the counter and began measuring the lace.

Corva stepped away to resume her shopping, figuring she could leave her paintings where they were until Vivian and Bebe left.

"I'm surprised she would dare to show her face today after the spectacle she made of herself yesterday."

Vivian's comment froze Corva in her spot.

"Yeah," Bebe added. "Can you imagine anyone being so nasty and unladylike?"

"She was covered with dirt from head to toe," Vivian went on.

Corva twisted, peeking at the sisters from the corner of her eye. They stood shoulder-to-shoulder, facing her rather than talking to each other. That was bad enough, but a middle-aged woman with a basket over her arm inched out from one of the aisles to see what the fuss was all about.

"And her hair," Vivian continued. "Why, it looks like a bird's nest in the best of times, but it looked positively wretched after that little stunt of hers."

"I'm sure she only did it to get attention." Bebe sniffed, raking Corva from head to toe. "Since she doesn't have anything else at all to recommend her."

"Ladies, please," Mr. Kline growled. "Not in my store."

Vivian whipped to face him, her eyes narrowed in a glare. "Excuse me, Mr. Kline, but doesn't my father own the deed to your store? Didn't he purchase it all those years ago when you thought you'd have to close or go bankrupt? Isn't he the one who invested thousands of dollars in this enterprise because you assured him you were as interested as he is in preventing Howard Haskell from monopolizing every business in town?"

The accusation made Corva's heart sink. It had never dawned on her that Bonneville could stretch his influence into businesses in town. There was no chance Mr. Kline would sell her paintings. Where half an hour ago she would have greeted that with relief, now, after the way Mr. Kline had praised her work, it was another crushing blow. But the blows had only begun to fall.

"I don't know why Franklin Haskell would ever lower himself to marry an unladylike nobody from who knows where," Vivian said, tilting her nose in the air.

"His aunt forced him to marry her," Bebe said, not to her sister, but to the middle-aged woman who was eavesdropping. "Franklin has always wanted to marry Vivian. It was his Aunt Virginia who sent away for this mouse because she felt sorry for her."

"Is that so?" The middle-aged woman pressed a hand to her chest.

"It's not," Corva murmured. She didn't have the confidence she needed behind her denial. The middle-aged woman blinked at her, then looked to the Bonneville sisters.

"It's true." Vivian nodded. "My father says that Virginia Piedmont must have threatened to disinherit Franklin if he didn't marry her." She waved at Corva with a dismissive gesture.

"Oh, my," the middle-aged woman said. "I wonder if Hetty Plover knows about this?"

Before Corva could say anything to prevent rumors from spreading, the middle-aged woman turned on her heel and dashed out of the store. Shocked and hurt beyond any blow her uncle had ever given her, Corva faced Vivian, fists clenched.

"That was unkind," she said, proud that at least for now, she had strength in her voice.

Vivian sniffed and shrugged. "So was marrying the man I wanted."

"Yeah," Bebe added. "And so was butting in and winning a baseball game that we were supposed to win."

"Franklin never wanted to marry you." Corva glared at Vivian. "And it's just a baseball game."

Vivian pulled herself up to her full height, the feathers on her hat quivering along with her honey curls. "That just goes to show what you know. In this town, baseball is never *just a game.*"

Bebe added a "Humph," and, "I told you she'd never fit in around here. And poor Franklin is stuck with a plain, unladylike nobody who shouldn't even be allowed to paint the side of a barn." She nodded to the two paintings leaning against the side of the counter.

For some reason, that final insult stung the hardest. Rather than crush her, like her uncle's abuse and cruelty had, the misery welling up from her soul filled her with iron.

"Well at least I'm not a pair of witless, overdressed cheaters who wouldn't know how to attract a man if their lives depended on it," she snapped. "Why exactly are all of you still unmarried, even with your father's money behind you?"

Her shot hit its mark. Vivian gasped, and Bebe squeaked in offense.

"I've never been so insulted in my life," Vivian roared.

"No? Just wait. I'm sure you'll collect a whole string of insults before long."

Vivian turned a dangerous shade of red, and Bebe's mouth dropped open. Corva had no interest in staying around to hear what kind of cruelty they would hurl at her next. She squared her shoulders and marched right past them, through the shop's door, and out into the street.

She had no idea where she was going, but with each

step away from the confrontation, her heart sank further. She *was* a nobody from nowhere. Franklin *had* been forced to marry her, in a way. She *had* behaved in an unladylike manner, and everyone in town knew her for that behavior. But she was so relieved to have escaped the nothing life she came from that who she used to be didn't matter. Franklin was kind and wonderful, and what they had shared last night was perfect. And the baseball game had been more fun than she'd ever had in her life.

Her drooping steps slowed, leaving her near the front porch of the Cattleman Hotel. Several benches and a wicker table and chairs dotted the porch, so as the last of her confidence and energy left her, Corva dragged herself up the porch stairs and collapsed into a heap on a bench. She buried her face in her hands and let herself weep.

She wasn't sure how long she sat there, stuck in her misery, before a man cleared his throat beside her. With a gasp, Corva snapped straight and looked up. The man in question was tall and thin, with white hair and an impeccably neat suit. His suit jacket bore the emblem of The Cattleman.

"I'm sorry." She wiped her eyes, rushing to stand. "I shouldn't be here, I know. I'm not a guest. I'll leave. I don't belong here."

Her final statement brought another wave of misery and accompanying tears. She sank back to the bench, eyes and nose streaming.

The white-haired gentleman took a pristine handkerchief from his inside pocket, sat beside her on the bench, and handed it to her. The simple act of kindness made Corva weep harder, but she took the handkerchief and blew her nose, dabbing her eyes. It smelled of clean laundry and faint cologne and warmth, like an embrace from the father she had lost so long ago.

"Would you care to tell me about it?" the man asked in a fatherly voice.

Corva shook her head, but then lifted her eyes to meet his. Something in their kind, blue depths pushed her to say, "I'm never going to fit in here. I'm not what a woman should be, and I don't deserve a man like Franklin."

The white-haired man balked, stiffening and leaning away. "Who told you that?"

A wave of sheepishness deflated her even more. "Vivian Bonneville."

He arched a brow. "I wouldn't go believing what that harpy says, or judging yourself by her definition of what a woman should be."

She knew he had a point, but it was still so, so hard to believe in herself.

"Maybe Franklin should have married her. She may be a harpy, but she's from a wealthy, respected family, just like Franklin. The most I can ever claim is that my father died a hero in the war."

The white-haired man continued to eye her with stalwart appraisal. "First of all, that's no small thing. Second, who was it before Vivian Bonneville who told you that you were worthless?"

Corva's sheepishness changed to prickles of both shame and wonder that this man, whose name she didn't even know, had seen right into her so clearly. She knew the answer to his question in an instant—her uncle—but she couldn't bring herself to so much as whisper his name.

The white-haired man took a breath and shook his head, resting his hand against Corva's back. "I was there when Mr. Garrett, Mrs. Piedmont, and Mrs. Evans came up with the idea of sending to Hurst Home for young women interested in marrying men here in Haskell and starting a new life."

Corva's brow shot up. "You were?"

He nodded. "I heard them discussing how Franklin Haskell needed someone special in his life."

She opened her mouth to protest, but he raised a finger to silence her and went on.

"Those three people care a great deal for Franklin Haskell. Virginia Piedmont has watched him grow from an impetuous and arrogant young man, to a broken spirit, to a young man full of promise, but haunted by his past. She cares for him like he is her own son. Do you truly think that she would send away for a bride for him who was anything but the finest, sweetest, and most suitable woman for him?"

Corva closed her mouth and swallowed, staring at the soggy handkerchief in her hands. "I hadn't considered that."

"Perhaps you should. Perhaps you're not used to it or have had to protect yourself in the past, but now you may want to consider putting your trust in other people, people who care about you and want to help you."

"Are there such people?" She lowered her eyes.

He paused before saying, "You're sitting next to one right now."

She shook her head. "You don't even know me."

"Do I have to be best friends with you to wish you well or to want to see you happy?"

Corva glanced up at him.

"No," he answered his own question. "But we're connected all the same. You're part of Haskell now, whether you can see it or not. You won so many hearts yesterday at that baseball game."

Heat infused her face. "What I did wasn't very ladylike."

He made a sound that was anything but gentlemanly. "That's Vivian Bonneville talking. Considering the example she set at the game, she shouldn't be pointing fingers. And if you think your behavior was shocking, you should spend more time with Virginia Piedmont. Or Lucy Faraday. Or Katie Murphy, for that matter."

Corva grinned as her few, colorful memories of those women who she had just met came to mind.

The white-haired man shook his head and squeezed her shoulder. "The point is, we're neighbors here in Haskell, not passersby or townspeople or faces in a crowd. With a few glaring exceptions, we take care of our own. We'll take care of you too."

The sentiment was enough to bring fresh tears to Corva's eyes. "I've never had neighbors like that before."

"Well, you do now." The white-haired man gave her shoulder one last squeeze, then stood, holding himself as stiff and tall as a statue.

Corva stood with him, biting her lip. "But what about Franklin? Marrying me wasn't his idea. And sometimes…sometimes he doesn't seem interested in me. He…he doesn't like my paintings."

"Your paintings? Are you an artist?"

She nodded.

The white-haired man paused in thought for a moment, then said, "How do you know he doesn't like your paintings? How do you know he's not interested in you?"

"He told me to take some paintings into town to sell them," she said. "And this morning, he was more interested in talking about cattle than…" She swallowed, a blush heating her cheeks.

The white-haired man let out quick breath. "Do me one favor, Mrs. Haskell."

She peeked up at him, heart and brow lifting.

"Before you tell yourself any stories about what your husband thinks or doesn't think, ask him."

"Oh, but I couldn't. What if he—"

"*Ask him,*" the white-haired man repeated. "I guarantee you'll be surprised with the answer."

She eyed him skeptically, but in spite of her worry, she felt as though a weight had been lifted from her shoulders. "I suppose you're right."

"I'm always right." He nodded. "That's why Mr. Garrett hired me to run his hotel. Now run along. If you're quick, you can make it home before lunch and have that conversation with your husband."

Confidence renewed, Corva nodded. "You're right. I need to ask questions first and panic later."

"Or hopefully not at all," the white-haired man added with a smile. "Now go."

Corva turned and hurried to the edge of the steps. At the last minute, she looked over her shoulder, half convinced that the man, whoever he was, would vanish, like some guardian angel sent to point her down the right path only to disappear. But he was still there, as real and solid as any other citizen of Haskell. His words stuck with her. She was part of something bigger than herself now, and if she needed it, help would be there for her.

Chapter Ten

As Franklin rode up to his house in the lengthening shadows of late afternoon, riding the horse he'd borrowed from his father's stable, a thousand thoughts cycled through his mind. No calves had gone missing that day, but one had been stillborn. Nothing out of the ordinary, all things considered. They hadn't heard anything from Bonneville all day, which was unexpected, but a good sign. Maybe the man knew when he was beat. His father had been in a grand mood all day, congratulation him, along with the rest of the team. He wanted Corva to come over for supper as soon as possible.

Corva.

Franklin sighed as he dismounted at his ramp and walked Kingsman into the barn to rest for the night. With all the business concerns pressing down on him, he'd still thought of his beautiful, clever, confusing wife all day. It had been nearly impossible not to replay the memory of their intimacies in bed any time he had a free moment, but those thoughts were superseded each time by worry about why she had looked so...so unhappy when he'd left. What had he done wrong now?

His Perfect Bride 145

Well, whatever it was, he would make up for it. If he couldn't make up for it with kind words and a smile, he would give her everything he had in bed. That thought renewed his smile several times over.

"Corva?" he called as he opened the front door.

She was waiting for him, sitting at the dining table in almost the same position she'd been in when he'd left that morning. A jolt of panic sizzled down his spine at the thought that she'd done nothing but sit there all day because of some shameful mistake he must have made. But no, there were subtle changes in the house. The scent of stew cooking wafted from the kitchen. The area of the fireplace—scene of the bath that never happened the night before—had been tidied further. The lamps had been refilled and their wicks trimmed, and they were lit to ward off the growing darkness. Some of her paintings were missing too, including the beautiful, sad picture of a woman in the rain.

Franklin paused inside the front door, removing his hat and hanging it and his cane on their pegs. "How was your day?"

She looked up at him, and right away there were questions in her eyes. Questions and something that burned with the intensity of a blaze. She hesitated for only a moment before hopping up from the table and coming over to him to take his coat.

"I went into town" she said, hanging it, then facing him. Her gaze fluttered down for a moment. "I ran into Vivian and Bebe Bonneville in Kline's store. They were their usual charming selves."

"I'm sorry." He raised a hand to squeeze her arm. That quickly turned into an embrace. He slipped his arms around her and held her close. One by one, the tight muscles of his back released. It felt so good to hold her, to have her to come home to.

Corva was stiff at first, but melted into him with an exhale. For a comforting moment, the two of them stood there together.

Then Corva leaned back, her brow knit in puzzlement. "Who is the white-haired gentleman at the Cattleman Hotel?"

Franklin's brow flew up. "Mr. Gunn? He's the hotel manager. He runs the entire place like a tight ship."

A smile spread across Corva's lips. "So he is real?"

In spite of himself, Franklin laughed. "Sometimes I wonder. He's so stiff and formal all the time."

"He's wonderful and kind and…and insightful."

Franklin blinked at her. Behind her smile, he could see flashes of deep emotion. "What happened?"

Corva peeled away from him and walked deeper into the room. "I was upset after my encounter with the Bonneville sisters. I ran out of the mercantile and found myself at the hotel. Mr. Gunn was there to…well, to talk me through things, to help me to see, to put things in perspective."

Franklin made a mental note to thank Theophilus Gunn the next time he saw the man. But at that moment, all of his attention was on Corva. She paused in the center of the room, then turned to face him. Her brow was knit again, and her lips pursed as if she had something to say.

"Franklin, why did you marry me if you didn't want to?"

He met her question with a surprised intake of breath. That quickly dipped to shame. He walked to the table, gripping the back of a chair for support. "Because Aunt Ginny wanted me to. Because I knew it was the right thing to do."

"Those are two different answers. Two *very* different answers." She wrung her hands in front of her.

If he could have done anything to take away the uncertainty and the pain in her eyes, he would have done it. "I'll admit, I was hesitant," he said, "but you have to understand. A long time ago, I proved that I'm...I'm not a very good person. I behaved selfishly. A lot of people could have been hurt. Mercifully, I was the only one who did get hurt. I was the one who deserved it."

"But Franklin, that was more than ten years ago." She stepped toward him, stopping again when she was only a few feet away. "Everyone changes in ten years, everyone. You're not that selfish, foolish boy anymore."

"No," he agreed, nodding. "But I am a man with severe limitations." He paused, rubbing a hand over his face and glancing down at his braces. "Look at me, Corva. Inside and outside, I'm a man in a cage." He tapped the top of one of his braces where it reached his thigh. "I do everything I can to keep myself in good shape, but I'm only going to get older, weaker. I never wanted to marry because I never wanted a woman to have to give up her life to take care of me."

A flash of frustration pinched her face. "But you're asking me to give up my life for you anyhow."

"I know, I—what?" He blinked up at her, sensing that the frustration pouring off of her now had nothing to do with his legs.

Corva huffed and took a step back. "We...we shared something special last night, and this morning you left without saying a word about it."

Franklin opened his mouth and raised a hand to defend himself, but nothing came out. He shifted his hand to rub the back of his neck. "I suppose I wasn't sure if you would want to talk about it. I never know what to say about anything that affects me so deeply."

Her expression shifted to hope. "It did?"

He lowered his arm and smiled sheepishly. "Of course it did. I'm not the kind of man who shares something that special with just anyone. After that, I wanted to share everything else with you. The mundane things too."

Of all things, she looked surprised. "But the girls out on the porch at Bonnie's in town…"

He chuckled, understanding dawning. "Bonnie's girls are sweet on any man who treats them with dignity and respect."

"They called you by your first name."

"It's a small town. Almost everyone calls everyone by their first name."

A rose-red flush came to Corva's cheeks. For a moment, she looked down, biting her lip. It was a surprisingly alluring gesture that heated Franklin's blood. But when she snapped up to look at him again, the frustration was back.

"Why are you in such a hurry to get rid of my paintings?"

He blinked rapidly, trying to catch up. "Get rid of them?"

Her hands formed fists at her sides, and her frustration turned to pure misery. "I know you don't like them, but every one of those paintings is a part of who I am, a part of my soul. I can't help it. If you hate them, that means you hate a part of me as well. If you hate a part of me, I don't see how this marriage could ever work."

"Corva." He stopped her before she could go on. "I love your paintings. I think they're wonderful."

"What?" She was so surprised that she backed up a

step. "But that first day, when I was painting outside, when I'd forgotten your lunch. A look came over your face as if you hated my work." She peeked to the side where the half-finished painting in question stood.

Franklin rubbed his face, looking sheepish. "I couldn't tell you then, but somehow you managed to start painting the exact spot where my accident happened all those years ago. I was thinking of that—of my stupidity, not of your skill. I'm sorry."

"But you told me to take them into Mr. Kline's store."

"I thought that you might want to sell them, or maybe display them somewhere so that people other than you and I could look at them. They're too good to hide away here."

"But I thought…"

Her shoulders dropped and her eyes lost their focus for a minute. Then she started to laugh. It was encouraging and unsettling at the same time. Franklin took a faltering step toward her as she gripped her sides and continued laughing. She glance up to him.

"And you don't think I'm too unladylike to be a good wife because of what happened at the baseball game yesterday either." It wasn't a question, but her eyes shone as if she needed an answer.

Franklin's lips twitched to a grin. "Corva, I've never been more proud of anyone in my life as I was at the way you stepped up and helped us to win that game. I never would have consented to play if it wasn't for you." He stepped closer to her still, almost close enough to reach for her. "And as for being unladylike?" A rush of desire flooded through him. "I've never wanted to hold or kiss or…do other things with a woman—a womanly woman— as I did the moment you slid into home."

Corva clasped her hands to her mouth, her blush

deepening, her eyes flashing. Then she lowered her arms and stepped into him, wrapping her arms around him as he closed her against him in a tight embrace.

"He was right," she said before he could kiss her.

Franklin's grin dropped. "Who?"

"Mr. Gunn." She laughed again. "He warned me to talk to you before jumping to conclusions about what you thought or how you see things."

Yes, Theophilus Gunn was definitely due for a gigantic thank you, possibly in the form of a check. "He's a brilliant man, isn't he?"

Corva nodded, but that was all she could manage before Franklin kissed her with a passion that practically lifted them off their feet. She felt so right in his arms, so complete pressed against him. Maybe it had been someone else's idea to bring Corva here, to Haskell, to marry him, but it was his idea and his alone to love her with his whole heart, for the rest of his days.

They stood their kissing for far longer than they should have. An urgency that was new to Franklin, but as old as time struck him, and he leaned back to whisper, "We should go straight to bed."

Corva gasped, her eyes sparkling. "I've got supper on the stove, just about ready to—"

A shattering crash broke through both his amorous mood and her domestic one. A brick clunked to a stop only a yard away from their feet. Corva gasped and crushed against him. Franklin held her tighter, following the line of the brick to the now broken window it had smashed through.

"What the—"

A second crash came from the bedroom, no doubt another brick.

"Stay here." Franklin let go of Corva, limping across the shattered glass to look out the window.

Twilight was falling, but he could still see the area around the house. A pair of horses stood many yards back from his barn. A flicker of movement and a flash of light came from the side. He twisted to see a man he vaguely recognized as one of Rex Bonneville's ranch hands…with something flaming in his hand.

"Think you can humiliate us?" the man bellowed. "Think you can spread rumors and show us up on the diamond?"

Before Franklin could respond, the man hurled the flaming thing in his hand. Franklin jerked out of the way as it shot through the broken window and shattered on the floor. A fountain of flame spewed up in its wake along with the stink of burning oil. Corva screamed with a terror that turned Franklin's blood to ice.

"Run!" He lurched toward the wall of flame that now separated them, but pulled back. Whatever the flammable substance in the bomb was, it had caught on the old carpet. The flames were growing instead of shrinking. "Run, Corva!"

She continued to scream, backing against the table, eyes so wide he could see the reflection not only of these flames, but of the flames that burned Atlanta in them. Another crash sounded from her bedroom. The sick glow of fire rose in both of the bedrooms now.

He had to act. Braces or no braces, he needed to use what strength was left in his legs. That was all that mattered. Steeling himself against the danger, he charged at the flames that separated him from his wife, his heart, his soul. A sharp lick of heat flared around him as he burst through and continued on to throw his arms around her.

"We have to get out of here," he told her, scooping his arm around her waist. "I can't carry you, so you're going to have to run."

She nodded, though her breath came in sharp, frantic pants. Franklin gripped her hand, searching for the safest way around the flames. They stretched almost all the way across the main room, but not quite. He set his path, then charged ahead, pulling her with him.

A thump sounded against the door just as they reached it. When Franklin tugged it open, he was met by a wall of flame. Corva screamed, and the two of them wheeled back. Panic began to inch its way up Franklin's back as he looked for another way out, but by some twist of luck or blessing, the flames around the door died down. The bomb Bonneville's man had thrown against the door didn't catch.

"This way." Franklin tightened his grip on Corva's hand and dashed forward. Glass crunched under their feet as they shot through the door and out into the cooling twilight. Far ahead of them, two men jumped on the horses that had been left to watch and rode off. There wasn't time to worry about them.

Franklin tugged Corva as far away from the house as he could before the coughing started. Then he stopped and doubled, racked with coughing. His iron braces were warm to the touch when his hands bumped them. Corva sank to the ground by his side, breathing heavily. They both turned to watch the house. Orange-red fire lit half of the windows, but the structure wasn't alight yet. There might still be time to save it.

As the thought struck him, Corva gasped, "My paintings!" Tears and terror streaked her face.

Franklin whipped back to the house. The fire was

spreading, but it wasn't too late. He still had a chance to do something, to save something. Without a second thought, he lunged forward, rushing back into the house.

Corva's mind clouded with every nightmare she'd experienced in the last ten years. All at once, she was that tiny, injured, and frightened little girl, running through a world on fire. The only thing that kept her from spinning out of control was Franklin's steady presence by her side. As they stumbled out into the cool grass, turning to watch the flames grow inside their home, the only thing she could think of were her blasted paintings.

And then Franklin ran back into the house.

"Franklin, no!"

In an instant, she snapped out of the fevered nightmares. The present and the reality of the situation—that her husband, a man she owed so much, a man she adored—had run back inside of a burning building for her.

"No!"

She jumped to her feet, stumbling toward the house. Franklin was injured. He couldn't move fast enough in a house full of flame to rescue a few pieces of canvas and paint. He was in danger.

She hesitated for only a heartbeat at the beginning of the ramp leading up to the front door. Heat spilled out of the house in waves. Inside, she could see flames licking up the walls, consuming the sofa. She thought she saw the dark shape of Franklin dash through the main room. A moment later, one of the intact windows opened and two of her paintings sailed out into the safety of the lawn.

"Franklin!" Corva shouted, and pushed inside of the house.

Fear closed in on her from every side. The infernal light all around her teased at the corners of her memory, conjuring the flames of Atlanta as well as the ones in Franklin's house. Across the room, Franklin yanked one of her larger paintings off the wall. He stumbled around the table—the corner of which was now in flame—and limped to the open window. Pain lined his face, but he pushed on.

"Franklin!"

He spun to her just as he tossed the large canvas out the window. "Corva? Get out of here, get out!"

"Leave them," she shouted. "Leave them and come with me."

"I won't let them burn," he called back over the roar of fire. "You love these paintings, and I love you."

Corva's chest squeezed with his declaration, with panic, and with the heat from the growing inferno. He loved her? He loved her!

"They're not worth it," she shouted. She jumped away from a flare of fire as one of the lamps shattered on the table. Sparks threatened to ignite the hem of her dress, but she danced away, putting out the flames before they could catch. The movement knocked her against the wall.

She gasped when her foot smacked against her paint box and easel. She'd left them there after bringing them in the other afternoon. As quickly as she could, she grabbed them and hurled them through the window that the brick had shattered. At least some part of her art would survive. That was the least of her worries, though.

She spun back to the room. Franklin was nowhere to be seen. "Franklin? Franklin!" He couldn't have rushed out of the house that fast, could he?

A thump at the far end of the room and a muffled cry was her answer. She dashed around the flames, searching for him. Sure enough, Franklin had fallen on the far side of the table. His face was contorted with a sharper pain than before. He thrashed his legs, and when he reached for one, his hands snapped back as if burned.

As if burned.

His braces must have been red hot.

Corva didn't call out to him. She didn't even think. With steely determination—far beyond the kind that had come over her when she ran the bases the day before—she sprinted through the wall of flames and around the table to him. He writhed in agony, jaw clenched over a scream. Smoke rose faintly from his trousers.

Without thinking, Corva grabbed him under his arms and tugged. She wasn't particularly strong, had never counted that as one of her talents, but in that moment, it was as if she had the strength of Hercules. She hoisted Franklin halfway to his feet, then turned and searched for the door. Flames blocked her from it, but they weren't severe. She would have to be fast.

There was no time to consider anything but getting Franklin out. Corva grunted and swayed into motion. Franklin growled, his body tensing with struggle as he did everything he could to move on his own and to shelter her. Time stood still as Corva half-dragged, half-helped him toward the door. They passed through a barrier of fire, and with another few, labored steps, they were outside. Franklin lurched to tug her away from the flames and down the ramp. Immediately, the air around them cooled, but the heat seemed to continue inside of her. The two of them plummeted to the dirt beside the ramp.

"Over here, over here," someone shouted.

Seconds later, Corva lost her hold on Franklin as something lifted her. She had the short, swift sensation of movement, then a thump and the cool of grass. Then water splashed all around her. A second later, she heard another splash and a sizzle, and Franklin crying out in agony.

"Someone get those off of him. They're burning up."

Corva turned to the familiar, urgent voice. Bit by bit, her mind focused on the world around her. Travis and Cody Montrose knelt on either side of Franklin, frantically working to remove his braces, jerking back and shaking their hands as the hot metal burned them. Franklin was soaking wet, his clothes singed in several spots. It was only when Corva rolled in an attempt to reach him that she saw her own dress was nothing but cinders below the knee. Water had been thrown on her to extinguish the fire.

"Franklin!" She fell into a fit of coughing as soon as his name was out.

"Corva," he answered through his own coughs.

He reached around Travis's back, hand extended to her. Corva dragged herself across the grass, only resting when her hand was firmly in his. He squeezed it, and then she blacked out.

Chapter Eleven

For the second time in his life, Franklin Haskell awoke in his childhood bed, wrapped in bandages and wracked with pain, after a disaster that nearly killed him. Only this time, his wife lay tucked against his side. He winced as he raised a hand to stroke her hair. Bits of it had been singed off, but that didn't make her any less beautiful to him.

She stirred, drawing in a breath as she awoke, then coughing hard enough to shake the bed. That set him off into a fit of his own coughing.

"This is the worst part," she gasped, voice wispy. "Dr. Meyers said it will go away eventually, but that we both inhaled a lot of smoke."

Franklin nodded, fighting to steady his lungs. They both managed to stop coughing, but it was an effort. Franklin settled for shifting to the side so that Corva could lay fully next to him and holding her hand.

At long last, he said, "You saved me," his voice cracking.

She shook her head. "They'd already seen the fire from your father's house by the time I ran in after you. The

Montrose brothers and Luke Chance rode like the wind to get here. Luke dragged us both out to safety, and the others put out as much of the fire as they could." She coughed for a few seconds before adding, "The house is ruined, though."

"That's not what I meant," Franklin wheezed. He slid his arm gently around Corva's shoulders, pulling her into an embrace. Her knee bumped his thigh, and even though it was nothing more than a gentle nudge, he winced in pain.

"Oh. I'm sorry, I'm sorry." She lifted to one arm, settling beside him without touching him.

That was the last thing he wanted. "It's nothing, just a little pain. I'm used to it. I'd rather hold you."

Corva glanced down at him, a doubtful twist to her lips. "Your legs were badly burned when your braces heated up in the fire."

"Even through my trousers?"

Corva nodded. "Do you want to see?"

He didn't. His legs had given him enough trouble to last a lifetime. But it was what Corva wanted. "All right."

Corva inched off the bed, then peeled back the sheet and quilt that covered him. Aside from a pair of drawers that had been cut short to leave his thighs free, he was naked from the waist down. The sight that met him was twisted and ugly...and he couldn't help but laugh.

"It's not that bad," Corva assured him even as his laughter turned to coughing that wracked him. "Dr. Meyers says there will probably be scars, but Aiden Murphy said he knows of a Cheyenne remedy for burns, and that if you rub it on your— What's so funny?"

Franklin reached for her hand, gesturing for her to sit on the bed again. As soon as his lungs cleared, he said,

"Along with the old scars, my legs look like checkerboards now."

Corva blinked, then looked at his legs again. Her brows rose, as if she saw what he saw. The old scars that he'd been left with after his first accident mostly ran up and down along his thighs and shins. The burn marks from his braces ran around his legs. His flesh was now a cheery plaid. A burn ointment had been applied to his flesh, giving it a sheen as though it was wet. She shook her head, then met his eyes.

"You do beat all, Franklin Haskell," she said. "Laughing over grievous bodily harm."

He hummed, fighting off another cough, and reached for her. She snuggled against him, careful not to touch his legs. It would have to be good enough for now.

"What about you? Are you injured at all?" His heart shuddered at the thought.

"No," she said, as if surprised. "My skirt burned nearly to ash, but Cody doused me before it could burn through my stockings. I've got a few small burns, but I'm actually fine." She finished with a long coughing fit. "Except for my lungs."

"Then kiss me." Franklin tightened his hold on her. "Kiss me before we start coughing again."

Corva grinned, then leaned over to brush her lips gently against his. It wasn't the kind of kiss he wanted. His body told him that it could be a while before he could kiss her the way he wanted. But for now, it would do. She was here, she was safe, and she was his.

"You saved me," he repeated, feeling the truth of it from the bottom of his heart.

She shook her head. "I told you, that was Luke."

He pressed his fingers to her lips before she could go on. "You asked me before the fire why I married you when marriage was the last thing I wanted. I don't know if I'll ever have the right answer to that question, but I can tell you this—whatever the reason, marrying you is the best decision I ever made. You saved me, Corva. You saved me from the sad, guilty person that I had become. You saved me from myself."

"I wouldn't say that I did all that." Her lips twitched into a grin, and her eyes filled with affection.

"I would." He rested a hand against the side of her face. "I still don't think I deserve you, but you make me want to try."

She curled her hand around his, pressing her cheek into his palm. "Even though I'm not a great beauty or a wealthy heiress? Even though I do unladylike things, like playing baseball or dragging my husband out of a burning building?"

He chuckled, heart blossoming to joy within him. "Because of those things, my darling. Because of all those things and more, I love you."

Her eyes grew suddenly glassy, and she whispered. "And I love you, Franklin Haskell. You're the bravest and strongest man I've ever known, and I'm proud to be your wife."

Her words took his breath away. He surged up to kiss her. She met him halfway, leaning into him as the temperature between them rose. Her ardor pushed him back into his pillow, and the rakish thought struck him that he might just enjoy staying on his back and letting her take the lead, once his strength returned.

They were still kissing when the bedroom door slapped open.

"I heard coughing in here. Is everything all—oh my!" His mother stood in the doorway, a hand slapped to her chest.

Corva jumped back with a gasp—which led to more coughing—and Franklin reached for the quilt to cover his legs…and other things.

A moment later, his father marched up behind his mother and looked into the room. "Feeling better?" he barked, and seeing the position Corva was in, said, "Ah. Yes, indeed!"

His mother hesitated for only a moment before throwing her hands up and coming all the way into the room. "At least it shows you're not permanently damaged."

"Of course, he's not." His father strode in and came to lean over the bed. "Broken bones couldn't take my boy down, and neither could a little fire. Next time we have a bad lightning storm, I should send him out to harness electricity."

"Please don't," his mother wailed, clutching her chest again.

"Dr. Meyers says you'll both be right as rain in a few days," Howard went on, more serious. "Your house is a ruin, though, so you'll be staying here for a while."

Franklin nodded. He wasn't terribly surprised. "As long as we can rebuild, I'll be happy."

"We can always rebuild," Corva said, and judging by the spark in her eyes, she meant far more than just a house. Between the two of them, they could rebuild their lives and make them a thousand times happier.

"All we need to do—" Howard started, but was cut off by a slamming door and a shout from downstairs.

"Haskell!" The voice belonged to Rex Bonneville.

Every bit of good feeling in the room evaporated. Howard marched back to the hall as Franklin pushed himself to sit, in spite of the stabbing pain it caused.

"How dare you invade my house, sir," Howard bellowed.

It did no good. Footfalls sounded on the stairs, and a moment later, Rex Bonneville was standing toe-to-toe in the hall outside of Franklin's open door. Only, instead of looking furious, Bonneville looked anxious, almost contrite. He spared one glance for Howard before turning and rushing into Franklin's room.

"How are you, my dear boy?"

Franklin was so startled by the man's question that he answered, "Well enough," before he could think better of it.

With a dramatic gesture, Bonneville sighed. "Thank the Lord in heaven above. We were all so worried about you. My girls have been beside themselves with concern."

Everyone else in the room fell silent, staring at the big, seemingly relieved, man. Corva backed all the way to the corner of the room, studying Bonneville through narrowed eyes.

Franklin was the first to recover his presence of mind. "What do you want?"

Bonneville gaped at him, as if hurt that his motives could be questioned. "Only to know that you are well. Can I get you anything? Anything at all?"

Franklin glanced to Corva. Her face was a mask of distrust. It was the right reaction.

"It was your men who set fire to my house," Franklin said, eyes narrowed.

"Yes, yes, I know, and you must forgive me." Through the appearance of contrition, Bonneville managed to emphasize the word *must*. "It was the new boys, Carver and Brecker. They were upset over the baseball game, you see. And Brecker is sweet on Vivian.

When he heard about the way your good wife insulted her in Kline's store…"

Bonneville glanced up at Corva, a snake-like snap of hate in his eyes. Corva swallowed and pressed herself further against the wall.

"Get out," Franklin ordered him without a second thought.

Bonneville flapped his jaws as if mortally offended. "I have only come to wish you a speedy recovery, and to let you know that the perpetrators have been fired and handed over to the authorities. I shall personally testify against them in court. And I assure you, nothing like this will ever happen again." His glance darted to Corva once more, then back to Franklin, and on to Howard. "Nothing like this will ever happen again, *am I right*?"

Whether he was talking about the baseball game or whatever Corva had said to Vivian at the mercantile, or whether he was harking all the way back to the talk about rustling, it was hard to tell. The message was loud and clear, though. War had been declared.

Howard cleared his throat. "Bonneville, I'll give you exactly ten seconds to get out of my house."

Bonneville's back straightened. "Is this the thanks I get for coming to wish an injured neighbor well?"

"One," Howard barked.

"If this is how you treat someone who has come on a mission of mercy—"

"Two," Franklin added, as loud as he could without coughing.

Bonneville scowled. "I see how it is. If I—"

"Three." Elizabeth took a step forward, glaring at him.

"I should have expected nothing less from this sort of—"

"FOUR." Corva launched out of her corner, adding, "Get out of our house, Mr. Bonneville," for good measure.

Bonneville gaped at her, his eyes popping. He stood there, looking like a bloated fish, until Franklin said, "Five."

"Fine!" Bonneville turned on his heel and marched past Howard and out into the hall. "But if you think this is the end of things, you are sadly mistaken."

He stomped off down the stairs, and the door slammed before anyone could say, "Six."

As soon as he was gone, everyone in the room let out a collective sigh of relief.

"He'll be trouble," Franklin spoke into the silence.

"Don't you worry about it." Howard stepped over to thump Franklin's shoulder. "You worry about healing up. You've got a ranch to help manage, a house to rebuild, and a family to start." He winked at Corva with his last statement.

"Howard!" Franklin's mother gasped.

"What? Lucy's already ahead of him by four children. He's got a lot of catching up to do, and I'm sure, as a Haskell, he's more than ready to give it a go."

"Yes, but you don't talk about it in public," Elizabeth hissed.

"Fine then." Howard laughed. "We'll leave the two of them alone."

Howard held out his hand to her, and Elizabeth muttered the whole way as she marched around Franklin's bed to take it. She sent Franklin a final look of tenderness over her shoulder before she and Howard left the room.

As soon as they were gone, Franklin and Corva burst into laughter. They managed to continue laughing without coughing for ten whole seconds. Corva sank to lay on the bed beside Franklin once more.

"Don't mind them," Franklin told her, hugging her close. "Dad will always talk like a rascal. You get used to it."

"As long as I have you, I could get used to anything." Corva smiled, throwing her arms around him. "And you'd better do as they all say and heal as fast as possible."

"Oh, yeah?"

"Yes." She lifted herself up enough to grin down at him. "Because they're right. We have a family to start. And I do believe we're going to enjoy ourselves as we start it."

"I believe you're right," Franklin said, quite certain that he'd never been so happy in his life.

Epilogue

The first chill of autumn was always a relief after a long hot summer. The change in the leaves that marked the season was one of the most beautiful things that Corva could think of every year. She'd tried before to capture the colors of fall on canvas, but this year, she was finally able to paint a picture that embodied everything she loved about the season. And among the red, orange, and gold leaves in the painting she'd so recently finished was something else that had recently been finished—a new house.

"What an excellent structure," Mr. Charlie Garrett complimented Corva and Franklin as they stood by a table laden with every kind of treat, all for the friends who had come to warm the new house. "I particularly like the way you've built the whole thing on one level."

"That was Gideon's idea." Franklin nodded to his brother-in-law across the room, who was busy keeping Minnie from using one of Franklin's canes as a sword to battle her little brother with. "I don't need as much help getting around as I was afraid I would after the burns,"

Franklin went on, "but it's still nice not to have to worry about stairs."

"I suppose that will be handy for you as well." Olivia Garrett winked at Corva.

Corva's cheeks burned bright pink, and she rested a hand on her barely rounded stomach. "I didn't think people knew yet."

"This is Haskell, Wyoming," Charlie laughed. "Everybody knows everything."

"Everybody knows everything about what?" Lucy bounced over to join the group, a baby on her hip.

"About everybody's business in town," Olivia laughed. "And you've just shown us all why."

"Because everybody is always talking about things all the time?" Lucy grinned.

"No, sis, because some people like to butt their noses into everyone's business." Franklin nudged her arm.

"Not everyone's business, just family business." She elbowed Franklin back.

Corva watched the exchange, her heart feeling light. So much had changed during the summer, in the months since the fire. Not only had Franklin recovered from his burns far better than anyone could have predicted, he'd learned to smile more, and he'd spent more time with his family. The Haskell family had always been close, as far as Corva knew, but throughout the summer, they had grown even closer. Franklin and Lucy got along so well, like a...well, they didn't use the expression "like a house on fire" in the Haskell family anymore.

"Do you know what else I know?" Lucy went on as everyone finished giggling.

"Ooh? What?" Corva asked. It was so easy to fit in with these people, especially Lucy, especially when there was town gossip to be had.

Lucy leaned in closer. "I've heard that several more of the ranch hands here on Paradise Ranch have asked Aunt Ginny and Josephine and you, Charlie, to bring brides out for them, now that they've seen how happy Franklin is."

"Is that so?" Franklin asked.

"It is," Charlie confirmed with a nod. "And Mrs. Breashears over in Hurst Home has let us know that several young women there are mighty interested in the job."

"So what are you going to do?" Corva asked, thinking of the friends she had made in her stay at Hurst Home.

"Why, we're going to find them suitable husbands, is what we're going to do," Charlie answered with a wink. "Seeing as we were so successful with our first try."

"I'm glad to hear it." Corva let out a sigh of relief. She wished that every woman who had been through what she had could have as happy an ending and as lovely a new start as she'd had.

"Well," Lucy leaned closer once more, "I've heard that a certain Mr. Luke Chance already has a bride lined up for him."

"Really?" Olivia glanced to her husband. "Have you three been looking for a bride for Luke?" She seemed more surprised than anything else.

"We have." Charlie nodded. "Although I can tell you, it's been no easy task."

"Luke is a good man," Franklin began, face slightly pinched, "but he's the last one I'd pick to be ready to settle down."

"Believe it or not, he was eager as could be when he approached us. I guess he's taking a page from Virginia's book," Charlie said.

"Well then, I hope that whatever young woman you pick is ready," Lucy said.

Charlie grinned from ear to ear. "From what Mrs. Breashears tells me of the young woman she's sending out this way, Luke had better be ready for her."

Corva's mind raced with all the possibilities of women who she'd gotten to know at Hurst Home. Whoever the lucky girl was, she didn't think they could possibly beat the level of happiness and satisfaction that she'd found with Franklin.

She stepped closer to Franklin, slipping her arm through his. "Whoever she is," she said. "I wish her all the love that we have found."

"I'm not sure that it's possible for a man to love a woman more than I love you," Franklin added in a whisper.

He bent closer to kiss Corva, in spite of all their friends standing around, and as her heart flooded with joy, it occurred to Corva that she didn't care one bit how unladylike it was. She loved her husband.

I hope you've enjoyed *His Perfect Bride*! Remember, reviews are always appreciated. And of course, there will be more brides. You can read all about Luke and his bride, Eden, in *His Dangerous Bride*, coming up next! Yep, Luke had better be ready, because Eden is not at all what he expected.

About the Author

I hope you have enjoyed *His Perfect Bride*. If you'd like to be the first to learn about when the new series comes out and more, please sign up for my newsletter here: http://eepurl.com/RQ-KX And remember, Read it, Review it, Share it! For a complete list of works by Merry Farmer with links, please visit http://wp.me/P5ttjb-14F.

Merry Farmer is an award-winning novelist who lives in suburban Philadelphia with her two cats, Butterfly and Torpedo. She has been writing since she was ten years old and realized one day that she didn't have to wait for the teacher to assign a creative writing project to write something. It was the best day of her life. She then went on to earn not one but two degrees in History so that she would always have something to write about. Her books have topped the Amazon and iBooks charts and have been named finalists in the prestigious RONE and Rom Com Reader's Crown awards.

You can email her at merryfarmer20@yahoo.com or follow her on Twitter @merryfarmer20.
Merry also has a blog, http://merryfarmer.net,
and a Facebook page, www.facebook.com/merryfarmerauthor

Acknowledgements

I owe a huge debt of gratitude to my awesome beta-readers, Caroline Lee and Jolene Stewart, for their suggestions and advice. And a big, big thanks to my editor, Cissie Patterson, for doing an outstanding job, as always, and for leaving hilarious comments throughout the manuscript. Also, a big round of applause for my marketing and promo team, Sara Benedict and Jessica Valliere.

And a special thank you to the Pioneer Hearts group! Do you love Western Historical Romance? Wanna come play with us? Become a member at https://www.facebook.com/groups/pioneerhearts/

Other Series by Merry Farmer

The Noble Hearts Trilogy
(Medieval Romance)

Montana Romance
(Historical Western Romance – 1890s)

Hot on the Trail
(Oregon Trail Romance – 1860s)

**The Brides of Paradise Ranch –
Spicy and Sweet Versions**
(Wyoming Western Historical Romance – 1870s)

Willow: Bride of Pennsylvania
(Part of the American Mail-Order Brides series)

Second Chances
(contemporary romance)

The Advisor
(Part of The Fabulous Dalton Boys trilogy)

New Church Inspiration
(Historical Inspirational Romance – 1880s)

Grace's Moon
(Science Fiction)

82728073R00102

Made in the USA
Middletown, DE
05 August 2018